THE
TALE-TELLER

A Novel by

SUSAN
GLICKMAN

Cormorant Books

for my daughter Rachel
and in memory of Sheldon Zitner,
who always played Prospero to my Miranda

Y anoche, mi madre
cuando me eché a acordar
soñabo un sueño
tan dulce era de contar:
que me adormía
y a orias del mar.

(Last night, mother dear,
when I lay down to sleep,
I dreamed a dream
so sweet to tell:
that I had fallen asleep
on the seashore.)

ONE

"La fortuna no viene sólo, kali buxcarla."
(Good luck doesn't arrive on its own; one must seek it.)

THE BOY THEY CALLED Jacques leaned over the ship's rail, squinting into the setting sun. There, shimmering in the distance, impossibly green against the pink evening sky, was New France. He inhaled in anticipation, and the welcome smell of earth and trees and grass and animals infused the salt spray he had been breathing for seventy-two days. He felt as though that relentless salt had scoured him inside and out, leaving him as raw as a peeled onion, and as full of secret tears.

It had not been a comfortable voyage. Like many of the other passengers, he'd developed a high fever within two weeks of boarding the *Saint Michel*. Unlike the ship's second mate and a prosperous silk-trader from Rouen, both of whom had been buried hastily at sea, the boy had recovered, but he had not regained the weight he'd lost during his illness. After a couple of attempts that left him choking, he found himself unable to palate the shipboard diet of salt pork, salt fish, and hard biscuits. Once they'd finally reached the Grand Banks and were able to purchase fresh fish his appetite returned, but until then — except for one welcome meal of chicken stew contrived after all the captain's laying hens had drowned — the boy had subsisted on peas, beans, rice, and watered-down wine.

Small and wiry, with dark eyes and olive skin, he appeared to be sixteen at most, having as yet no sign of a beard. He was quiet and kept to himself, politely deflecting all inquiries into his genealogy or his place of birth in France, the topics of most interest to the others on board. All he would reveal was that he was an orphan from a good family and knew how to read and write; however, because his older brothers had inherited all his family's land and money and he had no affinity for either the priesthood or the military, he had decided to make his fortune overseas. His memories of home were so painful he preferred not to dwell on them, allowing only that he had nearly died during the same typhus epidemic that had carried off his beloved mother. Was it any wonder he wished to start a new life in the New World, inscribing himself on a blank page of history?

He was not alone in this resolve. Though most of the *Saint Michel*'s passengers were indentured servants or soldiers going abroad for a fixed term of employment, there were about a dozen other immigrants paying for their own passage at a cost of thirty livres — at least two months' wages — apiece. This group consisted entirely of young men, though no one else was quite as young as Jacques. What was his trade, they wanted to know. He had apprenticed once to a baker and at another time to a tailor, so was handy at both occupations. He claimed to be very adaptable, and indeed whenever the sailors required an extra body on board he was the first to offer his help. The general consensus was that a nice lad like him should find employment easily; more easily than some of the rougher artisans such as the burly tanner from Bordeaux who persisted in giving Jacques loud and graphic instructions about how to seduce women.

Besides the tradesmen, soldiers, and servants, there were also several merchants and government officials travelling for business, an elite group who had paid one hundred and fifty livres each to eat at the captain's table and sleep in better quarters. There were only a handful of women aboard: the wives of a couple of the officials, who were rarely glimpsed by the general population of the ship, and a trio of nuns who had undertaken a holy mission to convert the heathens. The nuns resorted to prayer at the slightest hint of danger and kept resolutely away from the ribaldry and drinking of passengers like the irrepressible tanner, who seemed to enjoy embarrassing them. When not telling their rosaries or reading sacred texts, they were preoccupied with maintaining a semblance of modesty despite the absence of bathing facilities and the cramped conditions below deck. There was barely enough water to drink and cook with, and hygiene consisted mostly of rubbing a damp and stinking cloth across one's face. Not even the men stripped down entirely; no one ever got clean.

The quarters assigned to the lower-class passengers — a corner of the gunroom — were crowded and dismal. A sudden movement of the ship would fling the sleepers rudely on top of each other and, as most slept in clothes that were filthy and crawling with lice, this was an unpleasant way to be wakened. During one violent storm the occupant of an upper bunk, failing to scramble down in time, had vomited over Jacques's already fetid blankets. There was no possibility of acquiring fresh linens and the persistent smell made him gag, so he begged for permission to sleep elsewhere — anywhere else at all. He went so far as to ask permission to sleep in the nuns' corner, which was separated from the public barracks by a sheet of canvas, but the holy sisters would not agree to have any man, even a beardless boy, in their virgin territory.

Finally a vacant hammock was found in between decks with the crew, and thereafter Jacques had even less reason to socialize with the other passengers. Though he drank little and cursed less, he seemed to enjoy the company of the rough and rowdy sailors and said that he had dreamed all his life of undertaking such a voyage. When one of the other young tradesmen, a carpenter from Saint-Jean-de-Luz who cried himself to sleep each night, asked Jacques what he liked so much about being tossed up and down relentlessly and being cold and wet all the time, he replied that this was the greatest freedom he could imagine. Suspended between sea and sky in the cupped hands of God, he was free from the expectations of others. For the first time in his life he was only and truly the person he knew himself to be.

The carpenter was moved, despite his own misery, by

this uncharacteristically passionate speech, and wished Jacques would share his thoughts more often. The boy, however, preferred to ask questions of others rather than answer them himself. Nights when the weather was fair he could be found on deck listening to the sailors' conversation, eyes half closed against the fug of tobacco or fixed overhead, tracing the summer constellations. The Great and Little Bears shone brightest, welcoming him to the boreal forest, but just above the horizon lurked Camelopardalis, the Giraffe, as if taunting those who persisted in seeking a passage to the Orient by the Atlantic route.

The existence of this northwest passage was the cause of much animated discussion among the crew, some believing that it had yet to be found, some that it never would. Meanwhile, the inhabitants of the New World continued to bear the name of "Indians" given to them mistakenly by Columbus, though they were a different sort of people altogether. Jacques would often ask the crew penetrating questions, revealing that he had been paying careful attention to everything they said; moreover, he seemed remarkably well-informed for someone so young, particularly someone with no previous maritime experience. The boy was aware, for example, that an Englishman named John Hadley had recently invented an instrument for determining latitude which he called the "octant," even though the captain of the *Saint Michel*, the Sieur de Salaberry, did not own one, relying instead on the traditional backstaff. He also understood the principles of celestial navigation despite having never held an astrolabe, and often offered to stand at the stern of the ship counting the knots on the log-line to help calculate the speed of travel.

He was particularly interested in the mariners' tales of adventures in distant lands. No fact was too obscure, no story too outlandish to merit his attention. Everything fascinated him: the inadequacy of armaments on trading vessels as compared to those found on pirate ships, the prevalence of marriage between African women and French soldiers on the Guinea coast, the sordid particulars of the slave trade. Indeed, the main reason the sailors indulged his curiosity was that his questions made them understand their own experiences in strange new ways. They were so taken with the lad that they urged him to join the crew on the return voyage to France. He would make a good sailor, they said, given his affinity for all things maritime. But although he was flattered, he declined; at latitude forty-six degrees forty-nine minutes north and longitude seventy-one degrees thirteen minutes west this voyage would end. Soon he would step ashore in Quebec, a place whose very name, meaning "the narrowing of the waters," resonated in an alien tongue. And who knew what prospects awaited him there?

∽

WHEN THE *SAINT MICHEL* pulled into Quebec Harbour, a festive scene greeted its weary occupants. Ships of many builds and sizes filled the port, belying the French prejudice that the colonial enterprise was doomed to failure after a year plagued by cholera and crop failures. Some of these busy vessels were familiar — single-masted sloops, two-masted brigs, and even a four-masted barque — and some were not. The latter consisted of shallow wooden crafts being paddled along the shore, well away from the dangerous current, by Natives sitting so low within them that only their naked upper torsos showed. Gaping at the aboriginals, who manoeuvred with such nonchalant grace it seemed their canoes were fused to their bodies, the boy was reminded of the mythical Skiapodes of Pliny's *Natural History*, creatures with a single boat-like foot who were rumoured to inhabit India, Africa, and the "Terrae Incognitae": blank spaces on the map which had once included this very region. As more and more of the earth had become known, legendary monsters like these had proved elusive, casting doubt on ancient testimonials like that of Pliny, one of Jacques's favourite authors. Nonetheless he felt a thrill of excitement to be entering the heart of an unknown continent, where there was so much to explore. Where someone like him could become lost and, in the losing, find himself.

The rugged town was crowned with ramparts, its steep facade raked by stairs bustling with humanity. Green hills rolled away in the distance and the sun sparkled on the water. The panorama before him would have been impressive anywhere, at any time, but after so many weeks at sea it was brilliant beyond anything the boy could have expected. He pushed forward, eager to go ashore, but was stopped by one of the sailors who told him that before disembarking, all the passengers needed to get permission from a handsome man deep in conversation with Captain Salaberry. Though Salaberry had donned a blue overcoat and a clean linen shirt to celebrate his safe arrival, he was no match for the colonial official, resplendent in fur-trimmed brocade and lace as though he were welcoming the voyagers to court rather than to a busy port full of labouring stevedores and loitering boys.

The nuns, each with a cloth bag of missals slung around her neck, were the first to pass inspection, and nervously descended a swaying rope ladder into the waiting longboat. After them went a crate of tea and honey and chocolate and preserved fruit: gifts for their Canadian sisters, who they assumed would be pining for such luxuries after surviving on a meagre diet of roots and berries. The government officials were next, clutching their satchels of diplomatic papers and royal decrees, their pumps catching awkwardly at the fraying rungs. One stout functionary wearing a long red coat trimmed with gold braid momentarily lost his balance and, with it, his *tricorne* hat. The splash this object made hitting the water below was drowned out by his cry of dismay. A member of the crew below quickly fished the dripping thing out with his oar and offered it to its owner, who held it over the side of the boat as they paddled off. This being the land of inexhaustible beaver pelts, he was assured by those on board not to worry; he would soon be able to replace it.

The merchants, who had watched the discomfiture of the official with great amusement, were meant to follow in a second longboat, but they refused to leave until they saw their own precious cargo of guns and gunpowder, liquor, tobacco, blankets, cloth, cooking vessels, and assorted tools safely stowed on another conveyance. Then they too climbed down the ladder and the second longboat pulled away. Another rowed up and yet another, and the scene was repeated many times with the colonists and their dogs, their clothes, guns, household items and musical instruments, their portraits of loved ones and maps of the new land, until the only passenger left on the *Saint Michel* was Jacques.

He lifted his small bag of belongings expectantly, as though to throw it down to the waiting shuttle. Salaberry looked at the colonial official, who shook his head and beckoned Jacques to come over to them instead. The boy traversed the deck reluctantly, the Promised Land now shimmering in the distance like a mirage. He stood before the older men with eyes downcast, shoulders slumped, until the official grabbed him by the chin and pushed his face up into the light. The man ran his index finger along the boy's jaw as if testing the sharpness of a blade, then clucked his tongue.

"I shall be sending you to the medical examiner, I'm afraid," he said.

"Who are you?" asked the boy.

"I am Jean-Victor Varin de La Marre, Commissary of the Marine. But the more interesting question is: Who are *you*?"

"I am Jacques Lafargue."

"We shall see about that."

～

Today, the fifteenth of September, one thousand seven hundred thirty-eight, Esther Brandeau, aged about twenty years, appeared before us, the Commissary of the Marine, charged with policing the maritime population of Quebec; the aforementioned girl embarked at La Rochelle disguised as a boy passenger under the name of Jacques Lafargue, on the ship Saint Michel commanded by Le Sieur de Salaberry ...

— *From Jean-Victor Varin de La Marre to the Minister of the Marine in France.*

~

THE GIRL — TREMBLING WITH fear, her face ashen under its tan — was ushered by her captor into a room hung with rich tapestries. It smelled of candlewax and some kind of aromatic wood, and was stuffed with ornate furniture at least twenty-five years out of fashion. Before her stood two men, announced by Varin in a stage whisper as the Marquis Charles Beauharnois de La Boische, the Governor General of New France, and Gilles Hocquart, the Intendant. Recognizing the names of the ruling authorities of the colony, she bent forward at both knees and waist, executing an awkward compromise between a curtsy and a bow. Hocquart, a stout, balding man in sombre attire, began to smile before covering his mouth with one hand in an attempt to maintain a serious demeanour. Beauharnois, tall and thin and resplendent in satin and lace, saw nothing humorous in the situation; nor was he moved by the vulnerability of the slender neck revealed as the girl in boy's clothes swept her cap from her head.

"Why are you travelling in disguise?" Beauharnois asked brusquely.

"The only way I can explain is by telling you a story."

"Very well, then. We are listening," Hocquart said, sitting down at once on a comfortable sofa and motioning to his colleagues to do the same. Varin crossed to a blue guéridon side-table in one corner of the room, upon which pen and ink stood ready; Beauharnois chose a heavily gilded chair decorated with carved lion heads and lowered himself onto it with a great show of reluctance, crossing one silk-clad knee over the other, then fidgeting with his embroidered waistcoat, until he was forced to acknowledge that the others were waiting for him.

"Begin," he said. "Unlike the Intendant here, I don't have all day to waste."

The girl took a step forward, clasping her hands together in front of her and closing her eyes as though retrieving a distant memory, and in a surprisingly musical voice, pausing only occasionally while searching for the right words to describe a scene more accurately, told her audience the following tale.

TWO

"No me llores por ser prove, sino por ser solo."
(*Weep not for my poverty, but for my loneliness.*)

ONCE THERE WAS A green island in a blue sea: the greenest island, the bluest sea. At dawn the sun rose, a blaze of gold, over the horizon; at dusk white egrets stained themselves red as they flew through the sunset, dipping their beaks for the day's last catch. Quick fish darted through the water, playing hide and seek; crabs wrote mysterious names in the sand; apes frolicked in the trees. Each stone hunched around its secrets, each palm tree translated the wind, each flower held one creature or another. The entire island was alive with voices singing praise to the power that sustained them.

And then one night there was a terrible storm, with clamorous thunder and lightning brighter than the sun. The island creatures hid, for there was something out there they had not seen before — a structure of wood, with tall broken trees standing at its centre and enormous white wings flapping in the tempest. The thing rose and fell in the madly churning water. And from it came helpless cries, strangled by the wind and waves.

They understood the cries. And they were afraid.

Morning came, and with it the friendly sun shone on a beach made unfamiliar by a veil of wreckage. Tangled nets of seaweed, dead fish, a pulpy mass of octopus; tubes and ropes and the lid of a chest; a hat, a broken telescope, oranges and lemons. A Bible swirled face-down in the shallows, its cover two gilded fins, flapping. And something else: a tightly woven basket resembling the bottom half of a giant clam. From it came soft mewing sounds and a flutter of movement that enticed the apes from shelter. Slowly and fearfully they crept along the sand, still wary of hidden dangers.

The matriarch led them. Having lost her newborn two days previously, she was reckless with her own life. The tribe held back as she approached the object, then watched in amazement as she reached into it and brought out a small creature. Oddly hairless, it was yet remarkably like them: two round eyes on either side of the nose, lips sucking at the thumb on a clever primate hand. The creature seemed to recognize them too, giving the matriarch a toothless grin of welcome. Her lips curled in an answering smile as she placed the creature in her lap and began to search its head for lice.

In a few minutes, it was nursing contentedly at the matriarch's breast. The other apes gathered around, stroking the baby's cheeks with their long fingers; the young ones examined its toes, pale thighs, and dimpled knees and compared them to their own. Different yet the same, the way egrets differed from herons; it was not hard to understand. Though they had never seen another animal similar to themselves before, they could accept that such a thing might exist in this world of grace and abundance. For who knew what lay beyond their island? Water and sky stretched away infinitely in all directions and yet there were stories, passed on for generations, that their ancestors had come from another place, a place far away, and that one day the whole tribe would return to their home across the sea.

The child from the sea was a girl, so she was instructed in female ritual. Days had a steady rhythm: wake, forage for food, play, groom each other; nap, forage for food, play, groom each other. Each day was both like and unlike the others, for anything at all might happen: suddenly fruit was ripe and it was time for a feast; the next day they would all fast, mourning a young male poisoned by snakebite. She tried birds' eggs for the first time and liked them; she tried turtles' eggs and pronounced them foul. Crabs pinched, bees stung, butterflies tore apart in your curious hands, worms squished unpleasantly underfoot.

Mostly she was happy on her island home; mostly she fit in. Only one thing caused friction with the tribe and worry to her adoptive mother: the girl was fascinated by the ocean. She would spend hours wandering by herself up and down the shore, dancing in and out of the surf, making pretty patterns of shells on the beach, scooping out fistfuls of sand

and letting the water fill up her excavations. She loved wading in to her waist and letting the waves break over her head. She held her breath, plunged under, then jumped back up laughing, spitting salt from her mouth, shaking a spray of diamonds from her hair, while the apes yelped and covered their eyes with trembling hands.

The apes were afraid of the water and stayed away from it. They warned the girl about the danger she was in, pointing out the litter of dead creatures that washed up daily on their beach. They even punished her for her disobedience, withholding the choicest fruits and making her sleep by herself. But nothing worked; the sea continued to tempt her. And then one day a large wave carried the youngster beyond her depth, and she discovered, to her joy and amazement, that she could swim.

Unnatural! Declared the apes. Land creatures walked, sea creatures swam, and winged creatures flew!

"But what about the turtles?" asked the girl. "They lay their eggs on the sand and then return to the sea. What about the frogs and lizards who move back and forth from one element to another? There are other beings who inhabit both worlds. And you told me that I came to you from the sea, so maybe that is where I really belong."

The matriarch wept and scolded, but the girl was defiant. She spent more and more time alone, swimming along the shore, close enough to the island to come back in but far away enough to silence the disapproving voices of her tribe. Gradually the apes decided that she was mad and left her to her own devices — but, paradoxically, the less they opposed her, the more abandoned she felt. At least before she knew that, no matter how different she appeared, she was part of a family that cared about her. Now that they all seemed to agree that she didn't belong, she was lonelier than ever.

One day she ventured out farther than she intended, later than she ought to have been in the water. The sun sank quickly in that part of the world, and soon it became too dark to see the pale rippling line where the breakers met the shore. She had lost all sense of direction and though she swam for hours, the island got no nearer. Too tired to go on, she decided to float on her back until she regained her strength. Maybe she could rest all night and wait for the sun to come up and show her the way home. The stars had never seemed so far away or given so little light. All around her was impenetrable sea and silence. She was utterly alone.

How long she floated, salt tears mingling with salt water, she did not know. But eventually she heard something. She flipped onto her belly and saw faintly, in the distance, a dark shape moving towards her. It was as big as a whale! But it was clearly not natural — fire flickered at regular intervals along its looming sides, and silhouetted against the flames were shadows that moved and talked.

She cried out as loudly as she could, and immediately there was an answering shout. Figures grouped together under one of the dancing fires, threw something large into the water, climbed down into it, splashed towards her. She was pulled into a vessel by strong arms, wrapped in soft thick fibres, given something harsh and burning to drink that warmed her up at once but made her feel sick and dizzy. Then she slept and knew no more.

When she woke, the sun was already high in the sky and the island was nowhere to be seen. All around her were strange beings with hair around their mouths and on their chins but none on their cheeks, appearing to be halfway between herself and her ape family. They walked upright and covered their bodies with substances of many colours. Fascinated, she stroked the arm of one creature in something vividly blue, the leg of another in brown skins; someone else had pebbles down his front that glittered like the sun. She poked one, wondering what it was. The creatures laughed at her, not scornfully but kindly, as though she were a baby, then offered her some of their bright coverings and helped her put them on. The coverings scratched so much that she discarded them at once. However, the creatures showed by signs and sounds of disapproval that she must put them back on again. So she did. For they were generous, continually giving her things to eat and drink, washing her face with warm water, patting her head comfortingly, and she could see that they meant her no harm.

Soon she understood that she was on something called a "ship": an artificial island made of wood that moved from place to place, propelled by the wind and the unceasing labours of the people who had rescued her. These people came from a place called "Espagna" and they called her "Estrella" — Spanish for "star" — because they had found her shining white in the dark night. She was their changeling, their fairy child, their mermaid, their good luck charm. Because of her their voyage would be blessed. They were sure that they would sail home safely with their cargo and become rich beyond imagining.

The sailors tried to explain their way of life to her but

she was not used to human speech and, though she learned quickly, their ideas were so strange to her that she often misunderstood them. But she learned that though she was a "girl," she must pretend to be a "boy" if she wanted to stay with her new family, because girls were not allowed on ships. This she could not understand, but then, they could not understand how she could have been happy living with apes all these years. To them, her family was made up of stupid "animals"; they had no notion of the generosity and grace of the apes' way of life. She tried to explain to the sailors how similar it was to life on board the ship, how they all worked together, taking turns; how they all slept and ate communally. But they would hear of no such thing — indeed, the comparison was deeply offensive to them.

At last she stopped defending her former existence. Though she longed for the comfort of the matriarch's arms and the sympathy of her gentle black eyes, though she missed her brothers and sisters, she doubted she would ever see them again. She had no idea how far she was from her island, nor how to get back there. So she adapted herself to her new family, dressed herself as a "boy," and helped to run the "ship." After all, it had been a long time since she had been happy at home; maybe she would fit in better here.

"ALTHOUGH YOUR ELOQUENCE MAY take in more gullible folk, I refuse to play the *Jacques* — that is, the fool — in your *farce*," said Beauharnois, with a wry laugh which Varin immediately echoed.

The Governor General bared his yellow teeth at the girl, but she did not smile back. While telling her story she had seemed entranced — eyes hooded, watching pictures only she could see, her voice a low and melodious murmur, luring as a cello, comforting as water running over stones. As soon as she reached its conclusion, however, her confidence dissipated and she started chewing on her nails and shifting her weight from one foot to the other. This behaviour really did make her look somewhat ape-like, especially in combination with her tanned skin and thatch of thick dark hair.

"A few weeks in solitary confinement should persuade her to tell the truth, eh Hocquart?" he continued.

Tears filled the girl's eyes at once. She dashed them away with the back of one grubby hand, but soon gave up and let them fall freely. Her demeanour was defeated but nothing about her signalled guilt, only a profound grief she was too tired to hide.

Hocquart demurred; prison would not be necessary. She was only a girl, after all. Besides, the commissary was sure to find out everything they needed to know through his network of spies in France.

He had no doubt this was true. Jean-Victor Varin de La Marre was good at deciding who would be permitted to settle in the colony and who would not. He enjoyed the exercise of this power more than he should, and for that reason among others — his obsequiousness, his vanity — Hocquart did not trust him. Like many of the young men who flocked to the colony, Varin was consumed by the tapeworm of ambition. Which was why he would probably become rich one day, as such men do, and retire to a vast estate in France, surrounded by sycophants as opportunistic as he once was. It was a source of great bitterness to Hocquart that few of the officials surrounding him shared his commitment to New France. Even Beauharnois, vain as he was of his status as Governor General, was prouder of his hereditary title as a marquis — a title that had cost him no effort and signalled no accomplishment. Indeed, his most significant achievement in that role had been to waste his family's fortune.

"It was you who unmasked this minx, Varin?" Beauharnois asked. "I'm not surprised; I've heard that you have quite an eye for the ladies."

Varin nodded his head, trying to hide the smile on his face. He flattered himself that he was known as a bit of a roué, though no one was more notorious in that regard than the Governor General himself. Beauharnois's wife had not followed him across the ocean; it was common knowledge that they were estranged. Unencumbered by matrimony, he was free to seek the affections of every young — or not-so-young — woman willing to barter her body for advancement. It was surprising how many of those there were, even in a place as notoriously underpopulated with females as New France.

Beauharnois turned back to the girl and scrutinized her. Usually he undressed women mentally, a process made the more stimulating by its arduous length: unpinning the front of the stomacher from the robe and then pulling off the robe, unlacing the stomacher behind and letting it drop to the floor, pulling the outer petticoat off, removing the ridiculous panniers and the stays, stripping away the modesty skirt, and then at last, blessedly, the chemise …

But today was different; today he entertained the opposite fantasy, picturing the girl in front of him naked and shivering in a corner of the prison, lying on a pile of straw, her wrists tied together with coarse rope, and then dressing her elaborately, layer after layer, the better to undress her again at his pleasure. A futile exercise. Even clothed in the richest gown he could imagine, all gold brocade and pearls, this one would not be attractive enough to tempt him. So he resumed the interrogation impatiently.

"Tell me who you are and what brings you to New France. The colony may need more women, but we do not need more layabouts and liars."

"My name is Esther, Mon Seigneur," she replied. "And as for why I came here …" She stopped and glanced up at Beauharnois for a moment in mute appeal. But he looked so disdainful that she turned to Hocquart instead.

"The world has so become much bigger. Explorers keep discovering more and more countries that we did not even know existed. I wanted to visit some of them for myself."

"You disguised yourself as a boy in order to travel more freely?" Hocquart asked, fascinated.

"Yes, Mon Seigneur."

"Have you forgotten that under my authority you are a prisoner of the King of France?" Beauharnois broke in. He took a couple of steps towards the girl, who shrank back even further, her body flat against the wall.

"How could I ever forget?" she whispered, almost inaudibly.

Beauharnois turned his back on her contemptuously and started looking for his cloak. "More important engagements await me; I will leave your fate to the Intendant here. Hocquart, be scrupulous in your investigation of this person."

How dare Beauharnois condescend to him in his own house, and in front of that grinning social climber, Varin? It might be true that the palace of the Intendant was in the lower town while Beauharnois's chateau — like the manoir of the chronically absent Bishop — flaunted itself on the heights above. Even in New France society remained stratified, and the landscape echoed that arrangement neatly. Still, Hocquart's real power equalled that of his rival; indeed, one might say it exceeded that of the Governor General, which consisted mostly of representing the King by parading around looking grand.

Or so Hocquart told himself when, as was increasingly the case these days, the man's arrogance became insupportable.

"Marie-Thérèse," Hocquart called abruptly. His house-keeper, a wiry middle-aged woman with reddish hair pulled back tightly under a starched white cap, had clearly been eavesdropping outside the door, for she almost fell into the room. Recovering her balance she curtsied deeply, hiding the embarrassment Hocquart was too preoccupied to notice.

"Take this young woman to the servants' quarters. You can give her that empty storage closet as a bedchamber."

"Yes, Monsieur L'Intendant," she replied, staring curiously at the girl whose eloquence had thrilled her. What a small person she was to have undergone such an extraordinary adventure!

"Keep an eye on her," Beauharnois interjected. "Living with monkeys may have taught her all kinds of thievery." With that he pinched Esther's cheek, leaving a red mark that was swiftly absorbed by the flush that spread over her face and down her neck. Swirling his beaver-collared cloak about him, he gave an extravagant bow and swept from the room, Varin following like a well-trained spaniel.

THREE

"Quien no tiene su casa es vecino de todo el mundo."
(A person who has no home is everybody's neighbour.)

AS SOON AS VARIN closed the door behind him, the Intendant began coughing into his handkerchief. His asthma acted up whenever he was distressed — and he was extremely distressed. This situation was unprecedented. He had no idea what he ought to do with the strange creature who had washed up on his shore.

A lifelong bachelor and a career bureaucrat from the age of twelve, Gilles Hocquart had rarely been alone with a woman who wasn't a servant lighting his fire or serving his silent meal. His mother had died when he was eight years old, giving birth to a younger sister who joined her shortly thereafter — the third in a series of lost infants. In their grief,

Gilles and his father continued on quietly together without benefit of feminine companionship. It may have been that very lack of distraction which had made possible his steady progress through His Majesty's Department of the Marine to the powerful position he now held.

Luckily, the housekeeper continued to hover at the edge of his vision, awaiting further instruction, so he would simply leave the problem of how to handle the girl up to her. Marie-Thérèse was indispensable. Foreign dignitaries were expected for dinner? A word in her ear and an elegant dinner appeared. A case of wine was required to thank an army captain who had calmed panicky mobs during the cholera epidemic? It was delivered to the man's home that afternoon. A favourite book appeared to be missing from his library? Marie-Thérèse already knew exactly where he had left it, absent-mindedly, in another room, but had hesitated to replace it on the shelf until instructed to do so. The Intendant could not imagine functioning without her — indeed, could scarcely remember a time when he had.

"Marie-Thérèse, you will also show Esther where the bath is. And get her some women's clothes to wear."

"Certainly, Monsieur Hocquart."

He cleared his throat and turned his attention to his reluctant houseguest. "You ought to be ashamed of yourself, Mademoiselle, showing your legs in public!"

"Why?" she asked, as though it were not perfectly obvious.

For a moment Hocquart was taken aback. Why indeed? He looked down at his own spindly shanks, almost invisible beneath the swell of his middle-aged belly. Not for the first time, it occurred to him that silk stockings were not the most flattering attire for a man of his age. The habitants wore loose woollen leggings or trousers, both of which were warmer and more practical as well as less revealing. Maybe he should consider adopting the local fashion.

"It is a question of modesty, child. You are not among apes anymore."

"As you wish, Monsieur L'Intendant," she said.

Somehow this polite phrase sounded impertinent coming from her. Or perhaps he was being oversensitive, the encounter with Beauharnois having unsettled him as usual. Hocquart sighed, then dismissed the two women and settled down with relief behind his enormous desk, buried under papers, bills, legal suits, and royal proclamations. This desk was his native land, and the one where he felt most at home.

~

MARIE-THÉRÈSE LED THE GIRL to a bathroom at the rear of the long, two-storey building, clumping along in wooden *sabots* while the other trod silently behind her in men's boots of supple leather. A deep iron tub stood ready next to a bucket of rainwater, and a blackened kettle steamed away over a fire of enormous split logs. She turned her back on her charge as she filled the tub, motioning to the girl to strip off her filthy garments and throw them in a basket to be washed.

The girl undressed obediently, and Marie-Thérèse busied herself with the discarded garments. None were worth saving except for the leather boots. She decided at once that she would give them to Hocquart's stable boy, whose own worn-out shoes were held together with twine. The child would be thrilled to have a new pair and such a fine pair at that, though they might be too large for him. It was hard to say — he was perhaps twelve years old and this girl, though small and slight, was certainly much older.

"How old are you, Mademoiselle?" she asked over her shoulder.

"Nineteen."

"And is your name really Esther?"

"When you don't have a mother, how can you know your true name?"

"My poor child!" Marie-Thérèse said, turning around inadvertently at the profound note of grief in the girl's voice. She found herself gaping at the figure standing in the tub. Esther was thin and small-breasted, with bruised, sinewy limbs and bony hips. Her black hair was cropped and ragged and her thick eyebrows almost met above her nose. Indeed, there was little conventionally feminine about her, since most women her age plucked their brows and curled their tresses. If they were as slender as she was they disguised it deliberately, wearing garments that padded their bottoms and pushed up their breasts to redress the deficiencies of nature. Deprived of such assistance, Esther was a rough specimen indeed.

"I am ugly, aren't I?" she said sadly.

"Oh, forgive me; I didn't mean to stare!" Marie-Thérèse hastily replied. "I was thinking about your tale of life among the apes."

"So you heard it?"

"Monsieur Hocquart asked me to wait outside ..." Marie-Thérèse was so mortified that she couldn't complete the sentence.

But it seemed Esther did not mean to embarrass her; on the contrary, she asked, "Did you like it?"

"Yes, very much. You are a wonderful storyteller."

"Thank you." A radiant smile lit up the girl's face and in fact, at that moment, she looked quite pretty. "Now here is the important question: did you believe me?"

"If Monsieur Hocquart believes you, then I should too."

"Why?" The girl sat down in the water with a thud, spraying the housekeeper, who shrieked involuntarily. Marie-Thérèse mopped her face with her apron, while Esther scrubbed her own skin so roughly it seemed she meant to rub it right off.

"Because I am nothing but a servant."

"You are more than that, surely. Being a servant is what you do; it is not who you are. Nobody is just what other people say they are."

These words hit Marie-Thérèse with the force of a revelation. She thought at once of her father who, despite her tears and supplications, had sent her alone to this cold country because he had no dowry for her. She thought of the village boys jeering at the teeth that staggered through her mouth like broken fence posts. She remembered the priest who scolded her for being proud of her new bonnet and then put a sly hand on her bottom when she was weeping with shame. Nobody else had ever suggested that she might be more than a homely girl with no prospects. That a complete stranger might suspect she was — or could be — different than what she appeared to be was profoundly unsettling. That the person who thought this was completely naked made it all the more portentous. Clearly this girl's spirit was much larger than her body, so couldn't the same be true of anyone?

Having no idea how to reply, Marie-Thérèse reverted to servant mode, despite herself. "Well, you may be right," she conceded. "Now finish your bath while I find you some clean clothes."

∼

ESTHER LAY IN THE bath, finally, ecstatically alone. She felt like she was exhaling for the first time since she ran away from home. And after three months of hiding her body from others, sleeping between huge stinking men and washing only sketchily and in secret, clean hot water was a luxury she was in no haste to relinquish. If only she could stay here, dreaming of where she'd been and where she might go next, rather than facing the challenges that awaited her. For as much as she hated to admit it, even to herself, a life of adventure was more fun to imagine than to experience.

Her solitary childhood had given her ample time to imagine her escape; indeed, for years she'd dreamed of little else. She'd practically memorized *Le Télémaque, Le Solitaire Espagnol, Le Paysan Gentilhomme*, and many other works describing both real and fantastic voyages, including translations of *Gulliver's Travels* and her favourite book of all: *The Strange and Surprising Adventures of Robinson Crusoe, of York, Mariner*. Most people insisted that Defoe's book was a pack of lies but Esther didn't care; as a role model, Crusoe was more meaningful to her than Marco Polo, Amerigo Vespucci, or Henry Hudson.

The literature of travel gave her hope. If there were so many other worlds, maybe she could find a place where she belonged:

a place without arbitrary divisions between people based on where they were from, who their parents were, whether they were male or female. As a last resort, she dreamed of finding a desert island like Crusoe's, with fruit trees and friendly animals but without any visiting cannibals, where she would live happily on her own.

So she'd copied maps, and memorized trade routes, and studied the lives of famous explorers. A couple of times she'd even sneaked over the bridge and down to the docks to see the big ships that sailed up the river with cargoes of exotic goods from faraway places. She watched sailors load and unload silk and cotton and spices, coffee beans and cocoa beans and aromatic wood, filling warehouses with the wealth of the world: wealth her father was allowed to store for others but not to share in himself. As little as he cared about Esther, he certainly would have intervened had he known how his daughter was spending her days. But she was not in danger, for the mariners recognized in her a kindred spirit: defiant, lonely, and reckless. Someone with nothing to lose.

She stretched, feeling her tense muscles unknot. Her toes looked like a strange pink fringe waving from the end of her feet. She flexed them one by one: stunted country cousins to her aristocratic fingers, clumsy yokels unable to flourish a pen or wield a sword. Apes certainly had that advantage over humans; they could peel bananas with their feet. Esther tried to pick up a bar of soap with her own feet, but failed. It was too slippery and she was too tired to keep trying.

It was frustrating that her disguise had been so quickly discovered, for it would have been so much easier to continue living as a boy in New France. She hoped she wouldn't be sent home immediately; as arduous as the westward crossing had been, travelling against headwinds and through tempests, the return would be worse with winter coming on. And besides, having survived the journey, she wanted to explore her destination. She had to find some way of persuading the authorities to let her stay in this odd outpost with its silver candlesticks and baskets of woven grass, handmade lace and swamp-smelling mud.

She doubted she could win over the Marquis. She winced, remembering the contempt in his eyes: that old familiar contempt that told her she was utterly worthless. It made her feel tired in a way that the hard physical labour she'd undertaken on the *Saint Michel* never had. She wondered what it was about her the Governor General hated so much, her swarthy complexion or her meagre figure. Or was it that she had dared to dress as a boy? Something about Esther obviously repelled him even though he didn't know the whole truth yet. She must make sure he never learned it.

But Monsieur Hocquart was a different type altogether, less tyrannical, much more sympathetic; he had been entranced by her first story and would surely want to hear others. He had a kind of softness about him, an inwardness that meant he too had been wounded by life. She might succeed with the Intendant if she continued to appeal to his imagination.

≈

DINNER THAT NIGHT WAS onion soup, a fat roast duck with savoury carrots and beans, and stewed fruit. It was accompanied by a loaf of real bread and a bottle of fine Bordeaux, which Esther greatly appreciated after the crude *vin de table* served on board ship, a beverage so acidic it would have done better service polishing silver than quenching people's thirst. Even plain water tasted so good here: cold and clean and sweet, as though the distant ice-capped mountains she dreamed of visiting had been distilled into a glass. Esther had always loved food; her favourite place back home had been the kitchen, where she sought both sanctuary and comfort. She sighed, savouring both past and present pleasure.

"You have a healthy appetite, Mademoiselle," said Hocquart, who had watched in astonishment as his slender guest — now wearing a simple dress of brown wool with a creamy white collar and matching cuffs, her cropped hair tucked under a white cap — demolished second helpings of whatever she was offered. She was also drinking considerably more wine than he would have anticipated. They had sat uncomfortably opposite each other for some time, exchanging occasional comments about the food, he answering her questions about the number of people who lived in the colony, and of those how many lived in the city, and of those how many had been born here and how many were immigrants from France. The girl had inquired with genuine interest about which crops grew best in the local soil and which industries seemed most promising of future prosperity. She had been polite and intelligent but now it was Hocquart's turn to ask the questions; after all, he needed to determine her true identity in order to decide whether she ought to be allowed to remain in New France. He cleared his throat and began.

"You may not be a boy, but you certainly eat like one. None-theless, you did a bad thing, deceiving those who trusted you."

"How?" She looked up at him with a surprised expression on her face.

"Imagine how those who slept next to you will feel when they discover that their chamber-mate was a woman."

"But all we did was sleep like good children; we were so tired after a day at sea."

"Children are innocent," he snapped, frustrated by such obtuseness. "You are not."

"Only God can judge the innocence of my heart."

"Aha, you must be a Huguenot, as your name suggests." He smiled, gratified to have discovered something useful by his indirect method of interrogation. This revelation also made his decision simpler — the girl would have to be sent back to France, since Huguenots were banned from the colony.

"No, Mon Seigneur, I am not."

"Then if you are a good Catholic, you ought to be obedient to the authority of the Church and not disgrace yourself by such immodesty."

"But Joan of Arc dressed as a man and she is revered by all of France," Esther said, regretting the words as soon as they were out of her mouth. Pretending to be masculine had clearly liberated her speech as well as her actions; it felt like all the rebellious thoughts she had been suppressing for years were trying to break out at the same time. But it wouldn't do to antagonize her host so recklessly; he held her fate in his hands.

"How dare you compare yourself to La Pucelle?" Hocquart shouted, before giving in to a fit of coughing.

"Please forgive me, Monsieur Hocquart. I am not accustomed to drinking and the wine has made me speak foolishly."

Hocquart stared at her, baffled, trying to regain his own composure. This "Esther," whoever she really was, confounded all his expectations about the weaker sex. She was his prisoner, all alone in the New World, and still defiant. Such stubbornness inclined him to believe her story of being a feral child, for hadn't he been told that no ordinary woman could keep a secret?

He'd also been led to believe that women were abstemious in their habits and modest in their appetites, and she'd defied that expectation as well. Women were supposed to be deferential to men, leaving adventure and politics to them, passing their days in gossip and housework, music and embroidery, not undertaking ocean voyages. Was their passive behaviour merely a facade? Did they hide themselves in yards of fabric, layers of face-paint, and towering wigs so that no one could discern their true desires? Meeting this girl made him uncomfortably aware of his ignorance on the topic, which ordinarily was not a problem since he had so few dealings with the fair sex. But there sat Esther, a poor specimen perhaps but definitely female, tossed up on the shores of Quebec as she had once been on the island of the apes.

He winced at the memory of his own arrival so many years ago, which had been, in many ways, as disappointing as hers. The *Eléphant*, which had set out so bravely from France, ran aground at Île aux Grues and stuck fast. He had been compelled to splash through the frigid surf as the crew, running nimbly through the waves despite their cargo of cumbersome trunks and crates, snickered at his weakness. At one point he stubbed his toe on a hidden rock and fell, only to be rescued by a sinewy old tar twice his age. It had been the most shameful moment of his life. But the wreck of the *Eléphant* had also inspired him to the scheme that would redeem him: the scheme that would provide financial security for the colony, lure new immigrants from France, and make his name famous forever. He was determined to establish a shipbuilding industry in New France to produce the sturdiest and best-designed vessels to cross the Atlantic.

Hocquart realized suddenly that the girl was staring at him from under her thick dark brows. The girl from the sea.

Her story made him think of Botticelli's painting of Venus, floating on a shell clothed only by long golden hair — a reproduction of which he had studied throughout his adolescence, scarcely daring to hope that one day he might encounter such a figure in the pink and white, high-breasted, long-legged flesh. Of course Esther, with her sunburned face and scrawny figure, scarcely resembled that delectable goddess of love and beauty. Indeed, she scarcely resembled any sort of woman at all; it was amazing that Varin had been able to recognize that she was one! Still, her arrival here was as remarkable as it was unprecedented. Could she have been sent to him as some kind of omen? But an omen of *what*, that was the question. He had no idea.

FOUR

"Dame un grano de mazal,
y echame en las fundinas de la mar."
(Give me a bit of luck,
and throw me into the depths of the sea.)

RESTRICTED TO THE INTENDANT'S palace for three weeks now, Esther and Marie-Thérèse had developed a comfortable routine. During the day Esther stayed by the housekeeper's side and asked her innumerable questions about Quebec. According to the housekeeper, it was as close to heaven as she expected to get in this life. People treated her with respect here; that was the main thing. She, an illiterate country girl, commanded a staff of a dozen. The gentry knew her by name and all the merchants in the market bowed to her. Such a life would never have been possible back in France.

And she never went hungry — in fact, no one did here. The habitants were able to keep far more of their produce than her own family ever had on their miserable farm. In

France the peasantry hardly ever got meat, but here even the Natives could hunt and fish as much as they liked. The rivers teemed with fish; the forests with game; fruit and berries grew in abundance. Where others saw a howling wilderness, she saw the Garden of Eden.

Unfortunately for Esther, who was fascinated by the Natives and wanted to know everything about them, Marie-Thérèse knew remarkably little about those who had occupied this paradise before the French arrived with their copper pots and gunpowder, their wineglasses and smallpox. Marie-Thérèse had no Native friends, did not speak a word of any of their barbaric languages, and avoided them whenever possible. Having heard too many stories about Indians massacring saintly missionaries, the housekeeper was convinced that they might rise up at any moment and slaughter innocent Christians in their beds if the army didn't maintain strict control. And she disapproved strongly of the *coureurs de bois* who took Native wives and produced half-breed offspring. Besides undermining the Natives' respect for the French it wasn't fair to the children, who got left behind when their fathers returned to France, which they usually did.

Eventually Marie-Thérèse — though flattered at having her opinions taken so seriously — would tire of being interviewed and shoo Esther away, telling her that if she couldn't make herself useful she might as well go read a book, since the Intendant was kind enough to permit her to use his library. Then the strange girl would run off gratefully to the other side of the building, skirting the vast meeting room in which the Sovereign Council deliberated, and sit enraptured for hours until someone remembered to call her for dinner (which, after her first interview with Hocquart, she took with the servants). She was delighted to discover that Hocquart possessed French translations of many of her favourite books: Homer's *Odyssey*, Plutarch's *Lives*, Herodotus's *Histories*, Ptolemy's *Geography*, Mandeville's *Travels*, Hakluyt's *Voyages*, and many other tales by such as Leo Africanus, François Bernier, and Christopher Columbus. Clearly, under that fussy exterior, the Intendant had a romantic soul. She was lucky indeed to have ended up living here.

Despite her rapport with Marie-Thérèse, Esther remained shy with the rest of the household, saying almost nothing while they ate, listening intently to their gossip about daily life in New France. English traders at Hudson Bay were stealing all the best furs — there might be peace in Europe but skirmishes continued here, that's for sure. There was nothing to worry about; the Sieur de la Vérendrye and his sons were working hard to break the English monopoly. He was a hero, that one; a true patriot. Yes, unlike those greedy merchants from France, taking advantage of the poor habitants, suffering after a year of bad crops. It wasn't just the crops, it had been altogether an unlucky year: smallpox had broken out again and the church bells tolled steadily for the dead. And speaking of the church, where on earth was Bishop Dosquet? Had he abandoned them permanently?

Later in the evening, as she and Marie-Thérèse sat by the enormous hearth in the kitchen, the housekeeper busy with knitting needles or a crochet hook, it was Esther's turn to talk. Suspecting that whatever she said was being faithfully relayed to the authorities, she put in lots of details like longitude and latitude, number of days at sea, trade goods and their values, and the locations of various ports. She poured every single idea or image she thought might seduce her audience into each tale.

The first story she told Marie-Thérèse was what happened after her childhood rescue by the Spanish sailors.

~

I COULD PACE THE circuit of my island in two days but did not feel confined by it. Nature was so various there: the waterfall tumbling into the valley below, the beach of laying turtles and the beach of nesting birds, a meadow of lush white flowers and a cave crawling with poisonous snakes. Every place was different yet familiar, and I loved each more than ever once I had left it behind.

The *Santa Maria* was not a prison, but sometimes it felt like one in contrast with the paradise I had lost. It was a box with a base of ocean and a lid of sky, open to the weather. There was nowhere to go except around the deck or below it; nothing to see but scrubbed wood and shifting clouds and endlessly tossing water, the occasional flight of gulls or sleek grey back of a dolphin. I drew comfort from the familiar smell of earth and trees whenever we neared land. Nothing else broke the monotony of my first weeks on board.

In a way this was a good thing, as I moved in a new landscape of words, a cartographer of human speech. For though the apes were expressive creatures, among them communication was limited to immediate needs. Such statements as "Bad girl! Don't eat that!" or "I love you; come here so I can groom you," or "Where's the baby?" stretched their vocabulary of sound and gesture to the limit. They had no interest in knowledge for its own sake. In fact, the apes avoided thinking because for them mental activity — being solitary — was its own kind of prison. Who would wish to dwell among phantoms, alone, when she could be part of a warm and busy community? Who would wish to be trapped in her own mind when she could find comfort in someone else's arms?

With the apes I had lived a life of feelings, responding to the world through my body. We existed in the present, our awareness of past and future confined to anticipation and disappointment. We didn't expect to understand the causes of events or to influence them, so we didn't blame ourselves when things went wrong. Paradoxically, this brought us both anxiety, since the world was unpredictable, and peace, since nothing was our fault.

By contrast, the sailors of the *Santa Maria* experienced the unknown as a constant threat. Because the ocean was mysterious, they feared and respected it. Their lives depended on knowing which routes led to shelter and fresh water, where dangerous reefs of sharp coral lay, and how to avoid the whales' nursery or the shores of cannibal isles. Their minds were active all the time, adding fact to fact, subtracting error, multiplying by probability. Reasoning was no luxury for them.

Indeed, philosophical arguments often went on late into the night, while I lay in my hammock listening, rocking with the ship's motions as I once had been rocked by the wind in the trees. Despite the cabin's closeness and foul odour, the groans and snorts, farts and belches, and occasional nightmare shrieks of my companions, I liked sleeping with the crew. I felt safe there, as though I had a family again.

One of the sailors adopted me as a daughter. His name was Joaquin Fargo and he was a quiet fellow with a balding head, an asthmatic wheeze, and a long red scar crossing his face from his left cheek to above his right eyebrow. Joaquin had a wife and three grown children in Cadiz; his oldest daughter had married before he took off on this voyage and might, for all he knew, already be carrying his grandchild. And that child might even be walking before he ever laid eyes on it, if it lived past its first birthday.

He confided this to me with a kind of calm acceptance, as though he didn't mind missing most of the important events of his own life. As a matter of fact, he'd been at sea when all three of his children had been born and they hardly knew him. He kept promising his wife, Estella, that he would give up seafaring as soon as he had enough money to retire. They had plans to return to her father's village and buy a place with an orchard, a few goats, maybe even bees. What more does a man need but the blessed sun, a handful of olives, and fresh bread spread with honey?

But after a month or two on land Joaquin got restless. After two more, he found himself pacing the docks like a dog at the end of its chain. And a fortnight later, he'd have signed on for one last journey, poor Estella pleading from the shore, sympathetic tears in his own eyes but no ambivalence in his heart. Most of the sailors were just like him. I understood their dilemma, for I too had abandoned my family for the ocean's embrace. But what I could not understand, and they could not explain, was why there were no other females on board the ship; why — if what they said was true — there were no women on board ships anywhere.

How could I be the only one of my sex to be called by the water? I had been alone among the apes because of this obsession; now that I had found others who shared it, I was alone in a different way. Whenever the *Santa Maria* made port somewhere to trade goods or fill our dwindling food supply, I had to stay on board and hide as though there was something shameful about me. Joaquin insisted that I was being concealed for my own protection, but I didn't believe him. So sometimes I would peer over the side of the ship, wearing my boy's clothes, spying on the busy dockside life to see what other females looked like.

None of them resembled me in the least. They wrapped brilliantly patterned cloth around their bodies and occasionally their heads as well; ropes of beads hung on their necks and golden hoops shone in their ears. They laughed or quarrelled in high voices or sang sweetly to fat naked babies swinging on their hips. Some balanced baskets of food on their heads; some sat behind stalls of fruit, chanting prices to passers-by. And some nursed their children, baring breasts far larger than any I had ever seen on apes. Would I one day grow up to be like them? It didn't seem possible.

All around the calm brightness of the women, men sweated and swore, pulling ropes and heaving enormous boxes and bales of stuff. They were bigger than the females, and fiercer, and — especially when they got drunk, which was often — much louder. Some drank until they vomited, spewing greenish bile on the dock. Others passed out, groaning. Some sat lazily in the shade, smoking or playing gambling games. One time I saw such a game end badly, with a single flash of silver from a hidden knife. That time the puddle on the dock was red. I nearly fainted at the sight, so evidently I wasn't much like a man either. Was I always going to be different from those around me? Would I ever belong anywhere, or to anyone?

I confessed these fears to Joaquin. He listened with a serious expression on his face, nodded from time to time, but said nothing. Finally he asked me to sit on the bowsprit with him to watch the moon rise and he would tell me a story that might help. Someday, if you like, Marie-Thérèse, I will tell you that one.

OF COURSE THE HOUSEKEEPER wanted to hear the story right away, but at the same time enjoyed an unaccustomed feeling: anticipation. She recognized that waiting for the next instalment of Esther's tale would enhance her pleasure when she eventually heard it. Being entertained was a new experience for a woman whose whole life had consisted of labour. Now as she bustled about, her hands occupied with familiar duties, her mind replayed Esther's tale, reliving it with herself as the heroine. She mourned with Esther the loss of her childhood paradise. She scarcely knew what an ape looked like, having seen only an organ grinder's monkey at a fair, but she could imagine the wordless pleasure of animal communion by recalling her dear cat, Minou, back home on the farm. The drunken, gambling men were familiar to her, as were the nursing mothers and their babies. And she too had sailed on a big ship when she came to New France fifteen years before, so she could easily imagine Esther's life on board the *Santa Maria*.

Though many of the other passengers had been sick crossing the Atlantic, Marie-Thérèse had not. For the first time in her hardworking life she had nothing to do, so she had stood on deck for hours, gazing out at an ocean as unreadable as her own future. She, who had spent her youth fenced in as much by convention as by wooden barriers and stone walls, saw nothing around her but water and sky and perpetual movement. Clouds raced overhead; birds cried from unfathomably high and then plunged into the waves to emerge with flopping fish in their beaks. She felt so dizzy with freedom she imagined, for a moment, she might fly away with them.

That dream melted like snow in springtime once the daily routine of cooking, cleaning, and waiting on preoccupied men took over. Life in the New France — despite the occasional glimpse of an Indian clad in deerskins or a huge moose like a walking tree — was not much different from life in the old. She had been born to serve others. At least here her industriousness was rewarded, and she made her way quickly up the ladder of the household staff. But though Monsieur Hocquart was kind and treated her well, he rarely spoke to her except to give instructions. The laundress and the cook were both married and had very full lives outside the house; they chattered all day about their husbands and children and, in the cook's case, her grandchildren. They were polite to the housekeeper but rarely included her in the conversation.

Though she hadn't given much thought to it before, Marie-Thérèse now realized how lonely she had been until Esther arrived. The girl had become her constant companion and seemed to have no interest in making friends with the servants her own age. For their part, though they were curious about the visitor with the exotic history, the chamber and scullery maids were mainly interested in the boys who worked in the stable, on the grounds, or at the prison. But though all the boys were fascinated with Esther, she seemed invulnerable to their charms. She refused to flirt. She moved clumsily in the long gown she was now compelled to wear, frequently tripping over the hem, then holding it up too high and revealing more leg than was respectable. When Monsieur Hocquart admonished her for this behaviour, she retorted that he should try wearing a dress sometime and see how well he could move around in it. This comment shocked the poor man into complete silence and forced Marie-Thérèse to run out of the room, unable to suppress a fit of giggles at the thought of her portly employer laced into female dress.

Esther was as impatient with all recommendations pertaining to femininity as she was with her clothes. She didn't care how she looked, and rarely brushed her lustrous black hair. Exasperated, Marie-Thérèse would insist that the girl sit still while a comb was dragged through her knotted tresses; she would scrub at the girl's fingernails with the kitchen brush and pare them with the kitchen knife, muttering that, since Esther was as brown and dirty as a potato, she merited the same treatment as a potato.

One day, while she was subjecting her charge to this enforced *toilette,* Marie-Thérèse asked if she might have the tale she had been promised, the one that Joaquin told Esther on the ship. Esther agreed, and launched into her most elaborate narrative yet.

~

JOAQUIN TOLD ME THAT he had first gone to sea as a cabin boy, fifteen years old and as skinny as an anchovy. All the men in his family had been fishermen and lived their lives on the sea, but he was the first to venture any distance from the village, running away to Cadiz in pursuit of the beautiful brigantines they sometimes saw rounding the Straits of Gibraltar. Like those gallant ships, he longed to travel to the Atlantic and the mysterious lands beyond, lands of gold and silver and spice, of wild Indians and wilder mountains and forests. As soon as he was old enough, he ran away.

The first voyages were uneventful. The ships returned laden with sugar, nutmeg, cinnamon, and coffee from plantations in the West Indies, and smelled like paradise to a boy who'd grown up reeking of fish guts. He'd come home for two weeks each time, taller and stronger, with gifts for his family and a pocketful of cash. He'd become a man with capital and a trade, and was respected in the village. Even his fearful mother admitted that maybe his ambitions weren't unreasonable after all. Maybe a big ship was safer and more profitable than the fishing boats her other sons piloted; vessels which had already claimed the lives of her husband and her brother.

But the third trip was wrong from the start. When a boy he met on the docks told him that the *Imperio* would soon be leaving for the west coast of Africa, Joaquin signed on without a second thought. God would curse him for his ignorance. The crew proved to be miserable scoundrels, the captain a violent man eager to flog miscreants, and Joaquin spent the whole trip down the coast fingering his medallion of San Cristóbal, patron saint of travellers, and praying to be home again with his mother. When they reached Guinea things got worse, for the cargo loaded day after day for a month was no longer exotic foodstuffs but living beings: tall, graceful men and women with skin like burnished wood against which their scraps of rag and strings of bright beads glowed.

Begging for mercy, the Africans were driven with whips and guns into the belly of the ship. Men were shackled together on one side of the hold; women and children were crowded miserably, though unfettered, on the other. It stank of sweat and vomit and piss down there, worse than in the sailors' quarters, and the prisoners were rarely allowed on deck for a breath of fresh air. Nor was there enough water or rations for all of them. Some of the Africans arrived already starving or wounded, having been forced to march many miles from the interior; others became sick from the terrible conditions they were subjected to on the ship itself.

At last they left that cursed place and put out to sea. Joaquin hoped he would be able to distract himself with ordinary nautical activities but when they were only three days from shore, two people died. The first to go was a skeletal woman no one had known was pregnant who miscarried bloodily, her husband crying and reaching for her from the men's side of the hold; the second was an adolescent with a high fever, calling for his mother in the universal language of delirium. No sooner had they thrown his corpse overboard than a tropical storm blew up, sending huge waves crashing over the sides of the ship. The slaves screamed in their fetid prison while the crew scrambled frantically on deck. Being the youngest and most agile, Joaquin was sent crawling along the boom to lash down the sail. It swung wildly over the deck and then out over the water, where it flicked him off as easily as he might a mosquito from his sleeve. He was lost in the tossing dark. Those on board were too busy saving the ship and their cargo of bartered souls to worry about a single doomed cabin boy, and they abandoned him without a moment's thought.

Joaquin nearly passed out from the shock of the freezing water. He struggled, screaming for help whenever he got his head free of the churning waves, and then gave up, numbly resigned to the fate his mother had predicted. It was this he regretted most: that he had condemned his mother to spend the rest of her life alone in mourning black instead of dressing her in bright silks and getting her a housemaid as he'd intended. Before this last trip, he'd promised to buy her a talking parrot to keep her company. Indeed, he'd inquired among the crew for the likeliest place to purchase such a creature, but they'd simply mocked him.

These were his last thoughts before he woke only God knew how much later. His face was pressed into a litter of broken shells and the surf licked his feet like a dog trying to wake its master. He moved his limbs, tentatively. They hurt. It was possible his left leg was broken. But what was worse was that he could see nothing, nothing at all, even though his eyes were wide open. He passed his hands in front of his face; only a slight thrill of air confirmed that he had moved them. He blinked his eyes a few times; clearly the muscles still worked. He even touched his closed eyelids gingerly, one at a time. The orbs felt intact and firm as grapes. The lids were gritty with sand and fluttered instinctively at the pressure of his fingertips.

What would it mean to be blind? He thought of the raggedy, foul-smelling beggar man of his village who sat all day outside the church, yellow palms outstretched to receive the coins of passersby. Sometimes he sang or chanted in a melancholy monotone; sometimes he offered to pray for the souls of those who took pity upon him. If this were to be his life, Joaquin concluded that he would rather have died.

Or perhaps he was dead already and in Limbo, waiting for his designation in the afterlife. What did anyone know of Limbo, after all? That it was a borderland, as was this beach; that it was nowhere, as was this beach; that it was full of lost souls, as was this beach — at least, insofar as he was there, and as lost as any soul could be. For in truth, he had not the slightest idea where he ranked on the scale of human wickedness. In school, he had not recited the catechism with authentic fervour and had made fun of the adenoidal priest behind his back. As an adult he had refused to go to Mass with his mother; yet another way he'd disappointed her. In his last memory of her, she was standing fixed as a statue in the doorway, pleading with him not to go to sea. When he insisted that he had to go, she flung her apron over her head and started moaning that she would lose him as she had his father. Her behaviour had irritated him so much he'd left without kissing her goodbye. This was surely his worst sin.

For though he had filched oranges from his fat neighbour to the east and olives from his thin neighbour to the west, though he had told plenty of girls he loved them in order to steal kisses sweeter than oranges and more bitter than unripe olives, he had committed no major crimes. His conscience was clear of robbery, adultery, and murder, though there had been plenty of temptation — and opportunity (that freckled young wife behind the chicken coop, for example). And he'd been generous with what he had, sharing with others less fortunate even when he knew they couldn't pay him back.

Rehearsing these small villainies and smaller heroisms reminded Joaquin that one's whole life is supposed to flash before one's eyes at the moment of death. So I am dead! he thought, relieved to have at least one mystery resolved. Then he heard footsteps, and the next thing he knew, a gentle hand caressed his face and a woman's voice murmured something vaguely familiar close to his ear. His panic subsided, and he lay there waiting for his fate to unfold.

A wooden beaker was held to his lips and he drank the sweet water eagerly. The sodden remnants of his clothes were stripped from his body and his wounds were dressed with fragrant ointments. Then he was lifted onto some kind of hammock and carried, swaying between two poles, for a great distance.

How long he was carried he couldn't say, as he passed in and out of consciousness, lulled by exhaustion and the incessant movement of his conveyance. He could tell that the ground was rocky, and for a long time they definitely walked uphill. Once someone stumbled and he was almost dropped; when he cried out in pain and alarm, there was a flurry of apologetic voices in that vaguely familiar tongue. He also heard many birds; some, like seagulls, he recognized immediately; others were unknown to him. The wind sang in the trees, and when they moved into the open, the sun beat down on his unprotected face. He was everywhere and nowhere, saved and lost, alone among strangers.

Days might have passed, or hours. Time no longer had any meaning. There was only movement and then stillness; drinking and then sleeping. He had become an infant again, strapped to his mother's chest. He was oddly content in this unaccustomed passivity.

Eventually they entered a cool darkness. His hammock was suspended above ground to keep the weight off his injured leg, so that he continued to sway slightly as though his journey had not yet ended. Then someone spoke kindly to him and spooned thick soup into his mouth. It was full of some kind of grain, and beans, and chunks of tender fish, aromatically seasoned. Smelling of comfort, this was the best meal he had tasted since he left Spain, but he could eat only a little, his belly heaving from having swallowed so much salt water. His mind also was overwhelmed by his experience. Too exhausted to grapple further with the mystery of his rescuers' identity, he gave himself up to sleep, confident that he was among those who would not hurt him. Around him were the sounds of laughter, the high voices of women and children, and delicious smells. Wherever he was it was infinitely better than the floating hell of the *Imperio*.

Many days passed before he was well enough to get up, leaning on a stick because of his broken ankle, but he had not regained his vision. His hearing was unimpaired however, and it confirmed his impression that the language around him resembled Spanish, so he assumed that he must have been propelled by the storm to one of the American colonies. Indeed, the people acknowledged that they had heard of Spain and that Spanish ships came to the area occasionally. Maybe one day they could take him home. He was in no great rush to quit the hospitality of his rescuers, however, as he had grown fond of their quiet voices and sad music. That they preferred not to talk about who they were or where, exactly, their island was located, struck him as odd, but he attributed this reticence to their isolation, their primitive living conditions, and his own problems with communication.

As the days grew into weeks, he understood more of what was said to him and the others began to understand some of what he said to them. He learned that the place was called "Fogo" and the language, "Kriolu." He was convinced that he had been to this country before, perhaps in another life, or that he had sailed to one of those islands he'd read about in travellers' tales — a secret place that appeared out of the ocean mist every fifty years.

There was one girl in particular he became friendly with: the same one who had found him on the beach and saved his life. Her name was Aissata and she was sixteen, just like him, and had two big brothers, just like him, and her father was dead, just like his. She was the sister of his soul. He spent his days trying to think of ways to make her laugh, for the pleasure of hearing that silvery ripple of joy. Aissata's laughter redeemed him and made life seem worth living. Aissata's laughter promised that nothing bad could ever happen again.

And then one day when the wind off the ocean was brisk and cold, and Joaquin was helping the others carry armloads of firewood back to their cave, there was a sudden cry of alarm. It was quickly followed by the menacing crack of pistols and the smell of gunpowder and the fierce barking of dogs. Terrified, Joaquin clung to the side of the cave for support. All around him bodies swirled and eddied; running, fighting, falling. Strangers smelling of sour sweat and dirty beards pushed him aside roughly while the others were rounded up and dragged down the beach. A few small children were crying, but otherwise the people had become eerily silent. He kept shouting for help but no one answered him.

He recognized at once that the invaders were speaking Portuguese. They must be buccaneers, he thought, and here he was, defenceless. He had no weapon; he didn't even have eyes! Presumably they would execute him as soon as they had plundered whatever they could lay their hands on. They had only ignored him so far because, being blind, he had no obvious value to them. Joaquin crossed himself, said a quick prayer, and waited patiently for death, the death he had so recently outwitted, to find him at last.

To his surprise, one of the ruffians spoke to him in Spanish, asking if he was all right. Joaquin replied impatiently that he was more concerned about the others. The man laughed, and asked why he cared what happened to a bunch of black savages.

The others were black?

Yes, the man told him; they were runaway slaves who had been hiding in the hills but were now being returned to their masters where they belonged.

How could that be? They were kind, courteous people, nothing like the naked wretches he had glimpsed shackled below deck on the *Imperio,* screaming and moaning in an inhuman tongue. They ate proper food and made proper music. They were as civilized as any Spaniard he knew. More than most, perhaps. It was inconceivable.

His blood thundering in his ears so that he feared he would faint, Joaquin let himself be led to a boat anchored in the shallow bay. He felt the presence and heard the murmuring of many bodies on board, but did not reach out to them. He felt betrayed. Why didn't Aissata tell him that she was black? How could she make a fool of him like this?

On the other hand, he hadn't told her he was white. But he hadn't needed to; she could see that easily enough for herself. He was blind and, knowing he was blind, she had lied to him. She had tricked him into gratitude to her; no, more, let's be honest, into friendship with her. Maybe love.

He cringed when he remembered that he'd had fantasies of marrying her and taking her back to Spain with him. He had imagined the joy of his mother, discovering he was still alive, and her pride in his coming back with his lovely bride, the daughter she had dreamed of. They would have a big church wedding and invite the whole village and afterwards they would live with his mother, who would help with their children. Though sightless, he could still work for his brothers mending nets and maintaining boats, gutting and cleaning fish. He and Aissata would live a long and happy life together. That he had planned this phantom future with a miserable black slave made him sick to his stomach. His mother would doubtless prefer that he died here than come home with a woman like that!

But maybe Aissata didn't think of herself as "black" just as he didn't think of himself as "white." Colour was something other people saw. To herself, she was Aissata, his dear Aissata, as she had been to him until this moment. When he thought about her, who she was in herself, the words "black" and "slave" were meaningless. He had never been closer to anyone in his life than he had been to her.

He — who had prided himself on not thinking, but doing — thought something so new it made him shiver. Could it be that skin colour was meaningless? Perhaps it was no more significant than the colour of one's hair or eyes. His heart told him Aissata was as good as he was, even better. He knew she didn't deserve to be a slave and, if she didn't, maybe nobody did.

Joaquin sat in silence, the wind whipping at him, the salt spray rasping his skin, oblivious to the rest of the world. His mind grappled with ideas it had failed to confront through many wasted years of religious and secular instruction. What was the soul? Did it have anything to do with the body it was trapped in? If a person was truly good, did it really matter what race or religion they were? Only when someone offered him a skin of water and he spilled some, absentmindedly, all over his lap, was he roused from his meditations. Full of remorse, he called out for wildly for Aissata, declaring that he would save her, that he loved her, but the soldiers told him to shut up. When he wouldn't, they cuffed him on the ear and threatened to throw him overboard to the sharks. Only when they disembarked did Aissata's voice, her silvery voice, drift back to him, exhorting him to be free and enjoy his freedom for her sake. To remember her forever.

And then she was gone.

The officers took Joaquin back to their barracks where they insisted he don proper "European" clothes. Then they got him drunk. Until that day he had avoided alcohol, repulsed by the witless behaviour of his shipmates once they uncorked a bottle. But he now understood that there were things in life that would force a man to seek oblivion. Sometimes consciousness itself was unendurable.

The Spanish-speaking soldier thought he was drinking to celebrate his freedom and that he had finally come to his senses. He prophesied that in future, Joaquin would celebrate this as the day of his miraculous preservation. He would write a song about it. He could add another verse to the famous madrigal about Fogo: a tune Joaquin suddenly remembered having heard back home but hadn't connected with this Fogo, his Fogo, at the edge of the world. Where he'd been reborn.

The Andalusian merchant who returns
Laden with cochineal and china dishes,
Reports in Spain how strangely Fogo burns
Amidst an ocean full of flying fishes.

FIVE

"La hambre y el frio traen a la puerta del enemigo."
(Cold and hunger bring one to the enemy's door.)

ESTHER STOPPED SINGING AND stood up from the chair. Her hair shone, free of tangles; her nails were clean; her voice and imagination were both exhausted.

"And what happened then?" asked Marie-Thérèse, forgetting for once to cover her unfortunate teeth as her mouth hung open with amazement.

"Joaquin found a Spanish ship and he sailed home," Esther said.

"But that cannot be the end of the story! Because he wasn't blind anymore when you met him, was he?"

"No. Nothing slips by you, Marie-Thérèse. But I am tired of telling stories. All I want now is one of your beautiful *gallettes.*"

"They are for Monsieur Hocquart's supper. You know how much he loves sweets."

"But I do too!"

"Then make some yourself. Don't keep pretending that you don't know how."

Although Monsieur Hocquart employed a cook as well as two kitchen maids, having to entertain large groups often as well as enjoying good food on his own, Marie-Thérèse was accustomed to making the dessert: her specialty and his favourite part of the meal. And from occasional comments she had let fall, Esther had inadvertently revealed that she knew quite a bit about cooking herself, especially about making pastry. Reluctantly at first, but with growing enthusiasm, the girl revealed her talents. Her desire to please the Intendant and make herself indispensable to him prevailed over her aversion towards revealing anything significant about herself.

There were two unexpected advantages to Esther's new duties: Monsieur Hocquart had a good excuse for keeping her out of prison once she was usefully employed, and he finally allowed her to leave the grounds and go to the market with Marie-Thérèse. With its stables and bakery, prison and courthouse, the Intendant's compound comprised a miniature village, but a month confined within its boundaries had exhausted its novelty. Esther couldn't wait to see more of Quebec. And Quebec couldn't wait to see more of her, the girl about whom so many fantastic rumours swirled.

According to some, the feral child was half-animal, half-human, and had a face entirely covered with thick brown fur. She tore at raw meat with sharp fangs and, being far too savage to permit in the house, was kept in the stable, where even the horses were afraid of her. According to others she was dainty as a princess, spoke all the languages of the civilized world, played every instrument without book, and sang like an angel. The more credulous members of the community were disappointed when they finally encountered this mythic personage and saw only a small dark girl haggling over the price of butter. (Unlike most of the local bakers she preferred to use butter instead of lard in everything she made, insisting that the smell of pig fat spoiled fine patisserie.)

Sometimes they dallied on the way home from shopping to admire the flamboyant foliage: a ritual in Quebec, where everyone recognized that they would pay for each moment of transient beauty now with sensory abstinence in the months ahead. In October it was possible to see the world as God had intended it, all clarity and colour, each twig and leaf tip so sharp it could cut you from a distance, the air itself effervescent as wine. Esther said it reminded her of looking into the Mediterranean and seeing schools of golden fish. It gave her vertigo, knowing that she was looking up while simultaneously feeling that she was looking down. Height and depth reversed: the sublime and the profound indistinguishable, as though one's body had dissolved and its atoms were suspended lightly in space.

Marie-Thérèse never knew what to make of her charge when she spoke like this, but was pleased to see the girl happy. In fact one day, knowing how much Esther longed to visit new places and see new things, the housekeeper got permission from Monsieur Hocquart to give her a special treat. First they went down to the waterfront Esther had not revisited since the day of her arrival. After her arrest by Varin, the port — first glimpsed from the *Saint Michel* as the land of milk and honey — had turned turbulent and threatening, full of hostile men with loud voices leering at her. All she had seen was mud; all she had heard was meaningless clamour. Now a bright and busy scene met her eyes and she could enjoy the view across the harbour to Lévis. The sky was cloudless and blue, the river sparkling in the sun as they sailed east to the Île d'Orléans with a party of farmers and fishermen who passed the brief voyage singing familiar songs like "À la claire fontaine," and "Auprès de ma blonde." Esther was surprised when Marie-Thérèse joined in, her servile manner abandoned in the company of ordinary folk. Tentatively, Esther began to sing along too. For the first time since she had landed in New France not one person was suspicious of her and no one demanded to know who she was or where she was going. Such anonymity was freedom indeed.

When they came ashore, Marie-Thérèse hired a cart and driver to take them to a nearby farm that grew her favourite variety of apple, *Fameuse*, celebrated for its snowy white flesh. (Having grown up in Normandy, she had strong opinions about apples.) At the farm, they watched a boy picking their fruit until Esther — her spirits still soaring from the boat ride — asked if she might gather some herself. She clambered up as easily as if she were back on the rigging of the *Saint Michel* and refused to climb down until she had filled her basket with apples whose spicy perfume rivalled that of any flower. She also offered to make the dessert that night, producing an elegant tart which Monsieur Hocquart decided must be on the menu at least once a week thereafter.

Apple tart was not the dish her host prized most, however. That was chocolate. Esther was so fond of chocolate that she had brought a bag of cocoa beans with her from France, the discovery of which among her belongings puzzled Monsieur Varin, who did not recognize what they were. When she explained that they were something she liked to eat, he laughed and allowed her to keep them. Now that she knew what a gourmet Monsieur Hocquart was, she was especially happy not to have lost her treasure.

Marie-Thérèse watched with curiosity as the girl roasted a handful of cocoa beans in the oven, shelled them, and pounded them in a mortar to which she added two almonds and a hazelnut. She heated the resulting gritty mixture with sugar, water, a vanilla pod, a mixture of cinnamon and nutmeg, and one egg, whipping the thick liquid until it foamed with a wooden *moussoir* which she had also produced from her luggage. At last she poured the concoction into a cup and brought it in to Monsieur Hocquart.

He was delighted, proclaiming that Esther's chocolate was the finest he had ever tasted; better than the beverage served in the finest homes in France; better than that Beauharnois drank every morning for breakfast to give him stamina for his amorous and military conquests. Hocquart had often drunk chocolate at other people's houses but no one in his staff knew how to prepare it properly. Esther having revealed this talent, he would be happy to drink chocolate morning, noon, and night. He told Marie-Thérèse to inquire of the Governor

General's housekeeper where to procure the marvellous beans and also to buy the largest chocolate pot she could find, so that he could start serving the drink to his guests.

Meanwhile, Varin de La Marre had returned, more than once, as promised. Marie-Thérèse looked forward to his visits. Unlike Hocquart, who was flustered in the presence of women — even her — or Beauharnois, to whom she was no more than animate furniture, Varin contrived to be both amiable and insinuating, flattering the housekeeper, who in turn plied him with food and drink and delighted in his good appetite. He even asked for her advice about the fit of his clothes, as though a farm girl could be a suitable arbiter of gentlemen's fashions. She knew that Varin's initial report to the Minister of the Marine would not receive a response until the spring; no ship from France could make it back to Quebec before the port froze. So for now Esther was safe. She had shelter and food, and Marie-Thérèse had the pleasure of her company. What more could either of them ask for, or expect, given the girl's rebellious behaviour?

Esther herself kept her guard up. She had learned that she was less likely to get herself into trouble if she held her tongue so, in response to most of Varin's questions, she pled ignorance or simply shrugged. While acknowledging that she had travelled in disguise, she continued to maintain that her subterfuge was not malicious. Not having a sponsor or any local family, she couldn't have come to New France unless she pretended to be a boy, could she? And now that she was here, she didn't expect charity. She was strong; she would earn her keep. She assured him that she did not intend to become a burden on the colony or to be given any special privileges by the authorities. But Varin remained undeterred, if polite, in his interrogation.

"Brandeau, eh. Now where have I heard this name before? Some vineyard in Gascony, I think. You are from the south, then?" he asked.

"I sailed from La Rochelle on the *Saint Michel*."

"I asked where you were from, not where you boarded ship."

"I have told you, but you won't believe me."

"No one of sound mind would believe you," he said.

Esther took this as her cue to offer to make him a cup of chocolate, a welcome diversion for them both. She disappeared to the kitchen for the necessary time, returning with a small china cup of the precious stuff, then stood behind his chair while he drank it, positioning herself modestly as a servant, the capacity in which she hoped, for now, to be allowed to stay. Whenever he put down the cup, she immediately whipped up the foam again with her *moussoir*.

Varin complimented her on the confection, smacking his lips appreciatively after each sip, using a spoon to scrape up the sweet slurry at the bottom of the cup, but then reminded her that he would not give up the chase. Even as they sat comfortably chatting, his spies in France were ferreting out all her secrets. She might be able to seduce Hocquart by appealing to his appetite, which was as big as his belly, but she should not expect to succeed with him. Sooner or later he would find out everything. He always did.

"In fact, if I were in your position, Mademoiselle, I would exert myself more to impress someone like me. Someone who could be your advocate to the authorities, if he were persuaded of your sincere gratitude for his patronage."

"You speak in riddles, Monsieur Varin."

"And you tell lies. A match made in heaven."

"What do you want from me?"

"To be your guide in this New World."

"Thank you," she replied. "I appreciate the offer."

"I thought you would." He stood up, reached over and stroked the side of her face with one finger. An involuntary shiver passed over Esther's skin, which he quickly perceived. "A girl like you could learn many things from a man like me."

Esther walked away abruptly. "Apparently I misunderstood you, Monsieur Varin. I thought the subject of our study was to be this beautiful country."

"There is no limit to what we could discover together, my little Esther. It all depends on your aptitude as a pupil."

"It appears that the cost of lessons is more than I can afford."

Varin snorted impatiently, studying his reflection in a big gilt-framed mirror hanging over an equally rococo sideboard. He pulled down his tight-fitting green velvet jacket and adjusted his beaver hat to a jauntier angle. When he spoke again, all the gentleness had gone from his voice.

"I doubt it. We all know why girls run away from home. If you weren't so skinny, I would suspect you of being pregnant."

∾

SHE COULD ONLY HOPE that, armed with the few scraps of information he had, Varin would not be able to learn anything about her. No one back home knew where she was. All she had to do was continue to be "no one" herself, and they never would. Moreover, even if her so-called family somehow discovered that she'd managed to sail all the way to New France she doubted they would care. On the contrary, they would probably be happy. They could stop pretending she was one of them and stop looking for someone poor or old or disgraced enough to marry her. They'd done their duty, however unwillingly, and now they were as free of obligation to her as she was of affection for them.

And, despite the danger he represented, she had to admit that she too enjoyed Varin's visits. Sometimes he played the solemn officer of the law, sometimes the dashing young captain wooing the shy lass. And then he was the kindly older brother trying to comfort and protect his baby sister. With his confident masculinity on display, all broad shoulders, long legs, and seductive smiles, he was a welcome change from stout, self-conscious Hocquart and pious, subservient Marie-Thérèse.

Marie-Thérèse herself declared that Varin de La Marre was her favourite of all the young officers in Quebec. He had a gallant way about him that made her dream, sometimes, that one day she might find such a sweetheart for herself. They would marry, and Monsieur Hocquart, grateful for her years of faithful service, would give them a nice piece of land with good soil, and fruit trees, and a neat *allée* of oaks. On this land, they would build a house with a fine stone chimney, and she would hang lace curtains in each window and paint the front door a bright French blue, and they would buy a cow and a calf and a few geese and a flock of plump chickens and have three boys and three girls.

Once she'd confided this fantasy, Esther at first shook her head, then took the older woman's chapped red hands in hers and asked if that was really what would make her happy. When Marie-Thérèse said yes, the girl replied that she would pray that Marie-Thérèse got her wish, although she could think of no fate worse than spending the rest of her life cooking and cleaning and taking care of children. The world was so big, yet women's lives were so confined, declared Esther.

Such audacity astonished the housekeeper. How could any girl believe it possible for her to travel around the world as freely as a man? Esther's apparent conviction that she ought to be allowed to do whatever she wanted and go wherever she pleased inclined both Marie-Thérèse and Hocquart to believe her tales. That, and her horror of consuming animal flesh. (She said that, having been fostered by apes, she could not bring herself to devour any creature that nursed its young and therefore limited her diet to fish and fowl.) Why, she claimed to have visited Africa and Asia, the Americas, the Caribbean, and all sorts of exotic places Marie-Thérèse hadn't heard of, some with heathen names she couldn't hope to remember.

They were islands, mostly. Who would have thought there were so many of them everywhere? Before visiting the Île d'Orléans, the only island Marie-Thérèse had ever seen was Mont Saint Michel, which was only an island at high tide. So she had assumed that such clumps of land scattered around the water must be typical of a younger country than France. Those pieces would surely grow larger in time and join up with the mainland, like biscuits in the oven which grew bigger and bigger when they were heated, and fused together if you didn't leave enough space between them. But the Intendant had explained to her that the land itself was as old as France; it was only the buildings that were new. And now here was Esther declaring that there were islands everywhere, some small enough to walk around in an hour, some so vast it took days, but each one surrounded by water on all sides. Each one becalmed on the ocean, a boat going no place in particular.

~

AT THE BEGINNING OF November, Monsieur Hocquart informed Marie-Thérèse that she must work extra hard on polishing Esther's appearance. The Governor General — who had more or less ignored the girl since first meeting her — had suddenly demanded that she celebrate the feast day of Saint Charles, his namesake, at the Chateau Saint-Louis. The gentry were dying to see an authentic wild child, someone actually raised by beasts, he said; they could not believe their luck in having such a prodigy here, at this distant outpost of the empire. Even His Majesty Louis XV himself had no such phenomenon on display at Versailles; soon they might find the *beau monde* shipping out to Quebec for the privilege of viewing Esther, whom Hocquart, unimaginative paper-pusher that he was, took for granted.

Beauharnois's satirical inflection infuriated Hocquart, already burdened by the responsibility of managing Esther. He still wasn't sure what to do with her, nor what to believe about her. Clearly she was running away from something or someone she was afraid to tell him about, and that in itself made him feel protective of the girl despite his obligation to protect the state from whatever danger she was supposed to represent. At the same time he had no option but to accommodate the Marquis's summons, though he did remind the nobleman that, as Esther's guardian, he would be obliged to attend the festivities with her, to make sure she did not get into mischief — or worse, escape.

"Where could she escape to, I wonder?" Beauharnois retorted. "The wilderness? If we are to believe her tales, she'd be more comfortable with the savages out there than you are, Hocquart."

It was a sore point with Hocquart that Beauharnois, who spent four months each year in Montreal negotiating with the Indians, had quickly learned their tongue, while he continued to find it incomprehensible. Of course, the Governor General had been in New France much longer than he had, and the Intendant's office dealt almost exclusively with the civilian life of the colony. But neither the length of Hocquart's tenure nor the scope of his responsibilities was the problem. The simple fact was that His Majesty's loyal servant Gilles Hocquart was afraid of Indians. He feared their swift and silent agility, and their impassive faces observing those who had displaced them. The Indians were a threat to his faith in progress because, despite having encountered French civilization, they still preferred sleeping on the ground in animal skins to lying on soft featherbeds, and gnawing on leathery smoked fish and fried bread to forking up a nice moist salmon filet followed by airy meringues. He didn't understand them at all and what he didn't understand, he feared.

So Hocquart left dealing with them to Beauharnois, who loved asserting power in the name of King and country. Indeed, Hocquart professed to believe that half the money the Governor General requisitioned from the department of the Marine was to cover his extravagant wardrobe, not to pay his soldiers. Beauharnois was openly of the opinion that scarlet cloth and gold braid were essential weapons in subduing the Indians. He claimed that a tall man wearing a plumed hat and mounted on a gallant steed had the best chance of impressing primitive minds.

But when Esther, in a high-cut gown of blue silk damask, her shoulders covered with a mantle of the same stuff and her hair topped by a white lace cap, entered the ballroom of the Chateau Saint-Louis with Hocquart, it was obvious that Beauharnois himself was far from being the most extravagant dresser in New France. All the guests who crowded around him, hanging onto each syllable of his heroic exploits, were dressed in the height of Paris fashion. Despite the autumn chill, which the log fires burning at either end of the capacious ballroom failed to disperse, the women fluttered elaborate fans carved of ivory, mother-of-pearl, horn, wood, and tortoise-shell. Their powdered wigs were fantastically tall. Their bosoms, also heavily powdered, spilled over low-cut bodices covered in lace and pearls. Sleeves were ruched, or ruffled, or beribboned; skirts were hooped, or layered; nothing but the most brilliantly coloured fabric would do. The men too were resplendent in satin topcoats and embroidered waistcoats, lace stocks, silk stockings, and buckled court shoes. The colours were dazzling, and their onslaught on Esther's senses was rivalled only by the layered odours of perfume, hair lacquer, stale perspiration, tobacco, and wine.

Esther immediately pulled on Hocquart's arm and asked if they could leave. She was terrified of crowds, she said, and since she knew no one here, no one would miss her. So couldn't they slip away unobserved?

"No, don't be silly," he grumbled.

Seeing them hover at the edge of the room, Beauharnois opened his arms in welcome, his gesture taking in the flamboyant group surrounding him.

"Here is the wild child at last, come to entertain us over dinner with some of the fantastic stories I have been hearing — no doubt mangled in the retelling — from good old Hocquart."

Silence fell in the room as the two men stared at each other. Their rivalry was well known. They had fought over many things in the past; were they now going to fight over this strange runaway girl? The guests, growing more interested by the minute, pressed closer, their voices surging like the tide against a breakwater. Alarmed by the rising tension in the room, Esther overcame her nerves, stepped up to Beauharnois, and curtsied.

"What is it you wish me to tell you, Mon Seigneur?"

"Three simple things. Who you are, where you come from, and why you are here."

"My name is Esther. I do not know where I come from. And I am here to explore the New World."

This last comment evoked a huge guffaw from Beauharnois, which was echoed immediately by his followers.

"But you are just a girl!"

"As you are just a man."

"How dare you!" Beauharnois thundered, his hand going automatically to the silver hilt of his sword. All around him there were gasps of incredulity. Even Hocquart, at Esther's elbow, was muttering, "You must apologize at once," and she knew how much he hated his rival.

"I am very sorry if I have offended you, Mon Seigneur," Esther said, curtsying deeply, her face crimson and her eyes brimming with tears. "All I said was that that you are a man, as I am a girl."

"No. You said that I was 'just' a man. But I am Charles, Marquis Beauharnois de La Boische, le très haut et très puissant seigneur! How can you fail to recognize the power I have over you?"

The background murmur turned to excited clamour and Beauharnois had a sudden image of how foolish he must look, waving his sword over the head of a defenceless girl. A girl who looked as though she were about to collapse into the arms of Hocquart, that fat bastard. Hocquart was really enjoying playing the kind benefactor, wasn't he? Beauharnois would make him pay dearly for exploiting this moment of public awkwardness. The girl would pay, too. He wasn't taken in by her disingenuous facade for one minute; she knew exactly what she was doing. But if she wanted to play games, fine. He was an expert at playing games.

"But I keep forgetting that you grew up with apes," he declared, sheathing his weapon with an elaborate flourish. "Hocquart, if your protégée is to live among civilized people, she must be taught better manners."

"We are trying our best, Governor General, I assure you," replied Hocquart stiffly.

Beauharnois, consummate politician that he was, had managed to pull rank yet again. How did he get away with it? Though descended from old nobility he had no estate to speak of, so he had stolen his stepchildren's inheritance after abandoning their mother. This was public knowledge but nobody seemed to care. On the contrary; they admired the thief for his lavish parties and fancy clothes, and looked down on Hocquart, who had earned every sou himself. Well, fine then; if that is how shallow they were, let them look down on him. He did not intend to squander his hard-won wealth to impress people who persisted in living an idle life of balls and outings, an indoor life of flirtations and music and chess, as though they weren't a thousand leagues from France.

"And now, let us go in to supper. All this standing around in drafts is as bad for the ladies' complexions as it is for the men's digestions," Beauharnois declared.

His guests laughed on cue, relieved that the crisis had been solved, and the ladies sought the arms of their escorts to be helped into the dining room. Managing the trains of their gowns while balancing on high heels required some extra assistance. Esther watched them tottering off, fanning themselves and giggling coquettishly, with a sad expression on her face.

"I am not pretty, am I?" she said.

Hocquart was startled out of his thoughts. It hadn't occurred to him that the girl was conscious of her appearance, since she took so little care of it.

"Pretty is as pretty does, Esther. Do not compare yourself to these vain people; you have twice their brains, believe me. Now let us go eat."

SIX

"Las manos hacen, el Dios ayuda."
(Where hands work, God assists.)

LIVERIED FOOTMEN SHOWED THE guests to their places, where they stood politely until Beauharnois gave the signal to sit. Esther was placed on his right with an anxiously perspiring Hocquart next to her; across the table sat a vivacious woman named Madame Lévesque, whom the Governor General introduced as a descendent of one of the oldest families in the colony. Her ancestors had come over with Champlain and the Compagnie des Cent-Associés back in 1633 and settled one of the original seigneuries in the region. She was very wealthy and well-connected, Hocquart whispered; a good person to have on one's side, and he himself was very fond of her. It was easy to see why — despite her impressive lineage, the lady was no snob; on the contrary, she was very friendly, saying to Esther at once how much she was looking forward to hearing something of her extraordinary adventures, having lived a very dull life herself here in New France.

Madame Lévesque was accompanied by her husband, a doctor who was praised extravagantly by Beauharnois for his profound knowledge of human anatomy and physiology. Unlike most quacks, his repertoire of treatments extended beyond mere bleeding and purging, so he was the only person the Governor General trusted when he was ill. A dark and taciturn man, Doctor Lévesque spoke and ate little, in distinction to most of the guests, who clamoured with excitement as dish after dish was carried out by a series of pretty serving girls in sparkling white aprons and matching caps. The banquet commenced with a creamy soup of leeks and potatoes which was succeeded by trout poached in wine, a salad of dandelions and spinach, and suckling pig cooked in galantine. While Esther was still pondering this extraordinary concoction — a cold pâté consisting of ground pork wrapped in bacon, veal, nuts, and mushrooms, which Madame Lévesque explained had been sewn up in the piglet's skin before being baked slowly for twelve hours — a whole roast lamb was carried out on a spit by two boys, who paraded it around the room before carrying it to a sideboard to be carved. Clearly there was no shortage of food in the New World; equally clearly, no expense had been spared to make this meal as impressive as any to be found among the aristocracy in France.

When Beauharnois chided Esther for her rudeness in eating nothing but soup and fish, she explained that she was unaccustomed to such rich food, and in such quantities. She already felt unwell and could not possibly eat any more. Doctor Lévesque said that, like her, he was unable to digest anything too rich and suggested that she take a piece of bread to settle her stomach and make sure her wine was well diluted with water so that she did not get a headache. His wife remarked that Esther must have eaten much stranger things than this in her travels around the world. Did she still feel well enough to recount an adventure? Perhaps telling the other dinner guests a story might take her mind off her discomfort.

Esther hoped she was up to the challenge because she felt dizzy from the wine and was unnerved at being with so many strangers. Strangers who kept studying her as though she were an exhibit at a zoo, and talking about her as though they imagined she could not understand a word they said. When she'd entered the dining room she'd overheard one lady in an extravagantly beaded gown of yellow satin screech, in a voice as loud as any fishmonger's, that Esther was shockingly plain. Her companion, wearing several velvet patches on his face that failed to cover the ravages of smallpox, had replied that it was not surprising that the girl looked like a monkey since she had apparently been brought up by the beasts.

Their cruel laughter still echoed in her ears.

But Hocquart's eyes flickered back and forth between her and Beauharnois, reminding her that continued tenure in New France required the Governor General's co-operation, so she determined to please him in spite of their mutual mistrust.

She began hesitantly, "Once I made a soup from salt water and seaweed. That was quite disgusting."

"Where were you then, Mademoiselle?" asked a severe-looking fellow with a huge bony nose like an eagle's beak, and a monocle screwed into his left eye.

"On a rock somewhere in the middle of the Indian Ocean."

"Tell us the story at once, Esther. Obviously, you have a most attentive audience," Beauharnois said.

So Esther put down her fork, took a sip of water to clear her palate, closed her eyes as though to focus her memory, and told the following tale.

~

YOU ALREADY HEARD HOW I had been rescued from the sea by Spaniards. The ship that saved me was called the *Santa Maria*; the story I am about to tell took place after I had been on board for almost a year: long enough to feel comfortable hiding my body and revealing my thoughts, both of which had been difficult at first. In fact, as time went on, my limited stock of words lagged behind the increasing complexity of those ideas that came to me no longer in solitary bursts but all day long, in an interior monologue I was convinced others must be able to overhear. Indeed, my desire to talk became so fervent that my friend Joaquin insisted I was turning into a real woman after all. I wasn't sure whether I should be flattered or insulted by this comment, but I stored it away as one of many things to ponder at a later date when I had more experience of this brave new world.

I spent my time aboard the *Santa Maria* helping Joaquin and learning from him. Life on the ship was generally pleasant. The crew had been together a long time and were better fed and better paid than the sailors on most merchant vessels. This was because of the good management of the captain. He was willing to go almost anywhere and carry almost any cargo — except slaves. Captain Jago, whose own Moorish ancestry was betrayed by his dark complexion and tall stature, had forsworn trade in human lives, which was one of the reasons Joaquin was happy to serve under him.

One day, as we were heading towards the island of Madagascar to careen the ship and replenish our stock of food and water en route to the Orient and a cargo of ivory, silks, and spices, a square-rigged schooner flying a black and white flag bearing a skull and crossbones appeared out of nowhere. It gained on us quickly, revealing many guns on deck and mounted along the rails, and a crew of about fifty pirates. Captain Jago tried to escape, letting out more sail and throwing cargo overboard to lighten the load, but our clumsy merchant ship was no match for the vessel, especially once it began discharging its arms. The *Santa Maria* was not outfitted for serious battle, having but two cannons and one swivel gun. The pirates soon pulled alongside us, demanding that Captain Jago lower his longboat and come get them. This he did with alacrity. The captain had no more desire to make martyrs of his crew than he did to make slaves of innocent Africans, and he immediately surrendered all the gold on board in exchange for the pirate captain's solemn word that no one would be harmed.

The pirates proceeded to strip the *Santa Maria* of whatever they could find of value, including its pistols and gunpowder, wine and brandy, and a goodly stock of colourful cloth and mahogany from the African trade. No one was harmed, but several members of the crew were recruited to join their captors, me among them. Joaquin — insisting that he was my father — immediately asked if he could come too, and the pirates, perhaps mellowed by their easy conquest of the ship and its valuables, indulged him. They also commandeered the ship's cook, claiming that their own was incompetent, and our doctor, because medical skills are valued even among such ruffians. They then bid Captain Jago farewell, wished him a successful voyage, prayed that they might all raise a glass of rum together some day, and sailed away, firing a warning shot across the bows of the *Santa Maria* to discourage any pursuit.

The *Santa Maria*'s cook was a big man with a foul mouth who felt at home immediately. Although he drank as much wine as he poured into his stews, nobody reproached him for it because the more he drank, the better his cooking became. Our doctor spent his time reading and writing in his journal when not called upon to treat the venereal diseases, parasites, toothaches, and festering wounds that were the prevalent ailments on board. The pirates, thinking he must be bored, promised him that once they entered into battle he would be called upon to treat more bloody and interesting cases, and were surprised that he was not thrilled at the prospect.

This doctor, whose name was Esteban, was not an entirely selfish person. Concerned that the pirates might discover my identity and take advantage of me, he requested "the cabin boy" to be his assistant, and thus was able to keep me safe. The pirates teased Joaquin for making a girl of his "son" by letting him spend so much time with the doctor, but none of them suspected the truth until the day the revelation was forced upon them. It happened this way. You may have heard that in order to enforce honour among thieves, the crews of pirate ships are generally required to sign what they call "articles of regulation." On our new ship, these articles stipulated that every man would have an equal title to any provisions or liquor seized in the course of their criminal activities, sailors each receiving one share and officers one-and-a-half shares. They also included a list of piratical obligations, such as keeping arms clean and ready at all times, putting lights out by eight o'clock, and avoiding fighting amongst themselves, and of crimes punishable by marooning or death, including cheating any of the others, deserting the ship, or bringing women on board.

About a month after our capture we were asked to sign these articles, thereby becoming proper members of the crew. The cook signed immediately, seeing more profit under this new system of reward than anything available to him in his former employment. Doctor Esteban refused, saying that he hoped his services would be properly valued but he would not pretend he had joined such wicked company of his own free will. Joaquin merely asked why Captain Fergus's objection to women was so strong: a comment which, coming from such a homely figure, raised a shout of laughter and a host of obscene and insulting comments from the crew. Foolishly provoked, I in turn asked the Captain if any man who brought a woman on board would really be put to death. Captain Fergus looked at me with cold eyes, as though I was a parrot mimicking human speech, and simply responded "yes," whereupon I taunted him that he must therefore kill himself since I was a girl in disguise.

He drew his sword in rage. A murmur swelled around us as the crew absorbed this turn of events. I heard Joaquin behind me muttering, "Apologize; you must apologize at once!" But it was too late. Though I ought to have known better, I hadn't been able to resist saying what was in my heart, and would have to face the consequences.

Doctor Esteban stepped forward, attempting to appease the Captain by insisting that I wasn't technically a woman since I was not yet able to bear children. The captain sheathed his sword, muttering he would not be made a fool of, and that Esteban himself would be marooned along with me and my father as fitting punishment for his complicity in this charade. He called for blankets, and a tinderbox, and a jug of water and one of wine to be put into the longboat, as well as some ships' biscuit and a sack of dried peas. The doctor was given permission to bring his Bible and journal, though not his medical instruments. Joaquin had the foresight to request fishhooks and line and, after some consultation, was entrusted with a snarled length of twine and a few rusty hooks. Two large and heavily armed men forced us into the longboat and rowed out to a desolate island — not much more than a coral reef with a few mangroves stuck on it — where they abandoned us.

Contrary to all expectations our desert island proved kind. Though shark fins circled close enough to shore to prevent us from swimming, there appeared to be no poisonous snakes or large predators on land. We found enough wood to build a shelter from the tropical sun that beat down in unvarying brilliance day after day. Our only real challenge was constructing a storage system for rain so that we would not run short of drinking water. As for food, none of the local animals feared us at all, which made eating them seem unfair. Turtles and lizards lazed in the sun, blinking at us incuriously. Such quantities of fish browsed in the shallows that we could scoop them up with our bare hands. Some of the birds were flightless, and others were so untroubled by our presence that we could lift them right off their nests. One day, after we had not only consumed a mother frigate bird but also all the eggs upon which she had been brooding, I decided that I could not bear to devour one more innocent creature. That was the day of the seaweed and saltwater soup.

~

ESTHER BROKE OFF HER recitation at this point to sip some water from a crystal goblet. She held it up to the light to marvel at the prisms dancing across its facets, and appeared to forget her audience entirely.

"Esther, please. You can't stop now," exclaimed Madame Lévesque, sounding like a small child begging for another story at bedtime.

"But Madame Lévesque, I explained about the soup," Esther protested.

"Nonetheless, you have left your audience marooned on a desert island." Beauharnois was laughing; but, as usual, the merriment in his voice did not reach his eyes. "I order you to rescue them at once."

So Esther took a deep breath, closed her eyes again, and resumed weaving her spell.

∾

FOR FOUR MONTHS, BY Esteban's count, carved each sundown on the bark of a tall palm tree, we lived if not comfortably at least in relative safety. We named our sanctuary "Isla de las Tortugas," and as days stretched into weeks and existence began to seem less perilous, we began to understand the turtles' reluctance to exert themselves. There really was nothing to do except sleep, forage for food, and sleep again. The sun rose; the moon rose; the sun set. Once a school of dolphins came to play in the shallows and I overcame my fear of sharks to frolic with them. Another time we saw what might have been a ship, too far off to hail, shimmering on the horizon. The only work required of us was catching water and fortifying our shelter to withstand tempests.

I found the monotony of life on Tortugas familiar and was able to relax into its rhythm. But the men were restless, and soon began trying to build a raft large enough to take them to freedom. The first one they lashed together from branches and reeds was clearly too flimsy for the job, but they persisted. When the raft was torn to bits against the coral, they did not give up but scoured the island for stronger materials with which to build a more seaworthy vessel.

This obsession with being busy is one of the things I find peculiar about humanity. Apes are intelligent creatures, but they refuse to work more than is necessary for survival. They prefer to watch clouds billow across the sky or listen to the voices of the wind. Myself, I don't understand what it is about stillness humans find so unsettling. Perhaps they fear that a lack of motion indicates a lack of purpose. Or maybe repose too closely resembles death.

One day I asked Joaquin why he persisted in building a craft that could not survive the punishing waves of the ocean, should it ever manage to navigate the atoll. He retorted that being a sailor he needed to sail and sitting around idly waiting to be rescued was unmanly. Building the raft made the time pass more quickly and engaged his mind and his hands so that he did not despair. He insisted that I help him despite my misgivings, saying such work would keep me out of trouble, though what possible trouble I could get to in that remote and desolate place I never understood.

We had not completed the second raft when a real ship — three-masted, splendidly rigged with eight billowing sails — drew close enough to the atoll to notice us waving madly from shore. It was a heavily armed frigate. As it sailed towards us we discerned that it was flying the tricolour French flag. This worried Joaquin, who explained to me that France and Spain were traditional enemies, especially at sea. Luckily Esteban had a good working knowledge of French and was able to explain our unhappy situation to those on board. As soon as the captain of the ship understood that we had been marooned by pirates, he ordered the longboat to be sent for us, and we took our leave of the island of Tortugas.

Le Lys was well outfitted: more heavily armed than the *Santa Maria* because it was a navy vessel, but nonetheless more comfortable than the pirate ship. We were immediately offered hot food and clean clothes. That my new garments were far too large helped maintain the fiction that I was a boy. No one considered otherwise, which no longer surprised me. I had learned from my tenure with the pirates that most people tend to see exactly what they expect to see: no more, no less.

Esteban was happy to be our interpreter, asking as many questions as he answered about events in this isolated corner of the globe. It turned out that the captain, Le Chevalier Alphonse de Pontevez, was on a voyage funded by the King to claim new lands for France, and had named a fertile island northeast of Tortugas after himself. Pontevez was at first convinced he had discovered the original Garden of Eden, and anticipated starting a new French colony there, until *Le Lys* made berth on a less fortunate isle upon which they found broken chains and anchors and the wreck of an old French ship, the fate of which had long been a mystery. On shore lay the skeleton of a man shining white in the glare of the sun, rusted shackles loose around its bony ankles. Holding their swords before them like Archangels blocking re-entry to paradise, a search party spent two whole days exploring the interior of the island for any other signs of human occupation. They discovered several more skeletons and the ruins of a few primitive huts. Such desolation was more fearful in the midst of the exuberant green of creeping vegetation, the brilliantly coloured birds and flowers. The only mark man had left on the place was the sign of his defeat.

So the captain was perplexed about the true nature of these islands. Were they peaceful or deadly? Perhaps they were both, simultaneously. After all, the Garden of Eden had sheltered the satanic serpent, and the return of Adam and Eve to their first home .had been expressly forbidden by the Holy One himself. In this dilemma he was pleased to discover that three people — one of them an old man and one a mere youth — had managed to live for almost a hundred days in a place so remote, without proper food or shelter. Concluding that our survival was a good omen for the future of a French settlement that would carry his name to later generations, he declared the expedition a success and decided to sail back to France.

Once he had interviewed us and demanded that we draw as detailed a map as we could of our island, Pontevez ignored us for the rest of the journey. We were entrusted to the first mate, a cynical type named Fourget who spent most of his time sampling the Chevalier's excellent wine cellar and playing chess with Esteban in his cabin. Sitting with them day after day I began to learn French, as well as how to play the game of kings. Soon Joaquin and I had set up another chessboard and played alongside our medical companions.

"YOU AND I MUST play chess one of these days, Esther," interrupted Beauharnois. "Although somehow I feel the match has already begun."

"Governor General," Hocquart sputtered. "You asked the girl to finish her story. Please allow her to proceed uninterrupted or we shall be here all night."

"What can you possibly have at home that is so pressing you must leave early?" his rival replied. "Taxes to levy? Ships to build? Given that His Majesty is weary of supporting your fruitless schemes, my dear Intendant, you might as well stay here and enjoy the party."

In the momentary silence that followed Beauharnois's jibe, all eyes turned to Esther, hoping that she would end the impasse. She in turn looked at Hocquart, who nodded grimly, resolving to ignore Beauharnois's insults. It would not profit him to quarrel with the fellow in front of his cronies. She sighed and resumed her tale, glancing wistfully at the *franchipane,* a dense sweet tart made from ground almonds, sitting uneaten before her.

∾

ONCE ABOARD *LE LYS,* we sailed away from exile. Our first stop was Madagascar, to load up on provisions and give the crew a rest. The men spoke of it as a most enchanting place and were looking forward to shore leave with the greatest anticipation. You can imagine our horror when, at the entrance to the harbour, we were greeted by the decaying bodies of Captain Fergus and his first mate swinging on a gallows tree, a grim warning to any other pirates in the vicinity.

It turned out that shortly after we were marooned, Captain Fergus encountered a convoy of merchant marines returning from India. His crew tried to persuade him to flee, for it had a heavily armed guard, but being a deserter from the British navy, he had a score to settle with his former masters. Fate had pursued him across two oceans, he said, and it would be cowardly not to face it. Face it he did, with the result that time and distance were compressed into the span of the hangman's noose.

We learned the story from our old friend the cook, who had found a position at one of the taverns the crew of *Le Lys* visited on their leave. As soon as he saw Esteban, the cook ran to him, flung his arms around his neck, and told him how he was very lucky to have been marooned, as so many of the pirates had died in battle. When Esteban retorted that his own survival had never been assured, the cook insisted that he had known rescue would eventually come because the doctor was with the girl from the sea, who was a lucky charm.

Fourget was slow on the uptake, having drunk a whole bottle of wine and, luckily for me, he didn't understand the significance of what he had heard. Esteban quickly insisted they leave the establishment. As they walked, he told his befuddled companion an amazing story about his own early life, hoping to distract him before he figured out who the girl from the sea was.

Now I will share that story with you.

Esteban's father was an army officer stationed in the port city of Ceuta on the northern coast of Morocco. Ceuta was one of the last Spanish strongholds in the country and therefore under constant siege from the armies of the notorious tyrant, Sultan Moulay Ismail. Because it was considered a dangerous posting, they had a beautiful house and many servants. Despite this relative luxury, Esteban's mother was terribly homesick. She missed her mother and sisters and hated being stuck in a miserable heathen outpost with her young husband and little boy. Seeking consolation, she frequently left Esteban at home with his nurse, Edza, while she went out shopping in the bazaar or drank tea with the other officers' wives. For this reason, the boy gradually became more attached to Edza than to his own mother.

One day, while they were playing marbles in the courtyard, a Berber tribesman came to the door selling carpets. Edza tried to send him away but the man pushed past her through the gate and quickly unrolled a beautiful carpet, singing its praises in a loud voice. According to the Moorish fashion, the courtyard was covered with tiles of azure and white upon which the carpet floated like a treasure island, all gold and crimson. The sweet murmur of water from the fountain accompanied the boy as he danced around happily, while Edza yelled at him to stop, for if he got the Berber's property dirty she would be compelled to buy it.

Eventually she succeeded in grabbing Esteban and called loudly for somebody to come expel the intruder. But no one came to her assistance. Instead, three large men with scimitars burst through the doorway and grabbed the child and his nurse, rolled them up in the carpet, and carried them on their shoulders out to a waiting donkey cart. The frightened prisoners were flung into the back of the cart, wrapped together as tightly as cheese and spinach inside those tasty pastries Moroccan Jews call *bourekas*. On the one hand, they felt like they were suffocating and their faces were as scratched and sore as if they had been dragged across the desert sands, but on the other, the carpet protected them as they left the city for a long bumpy ride through the Rif mountains to the south.

They stopped for the night at the home of the carpet-weaver, a miserable clay hut in the middle of nowhere. His wife and three daughters waited on them hand and foot as though they were honoured guests and not prisoners, washing their feet and apologizing for the uncomfortable journey, feeding them until they could eat no more. After supper, the women of the family were sent out of the room and the men started asking questions. They were especially anxious to know if the Europeans feared the armies of the great Sultan Moulay Ismail, whose very name seemed to fill them with terror, so that they looked over their shoulders to see if any spy lurked in the shadowy corners of the hovel or under the stunted olive trees outside its door. They could not believe that their prisoners were unfamiliar with this prodigy but in the course of their questioning they found out why. To their dismay, they discovered that Edza was an Arab servant and not the wife of an important Spanish official. They assumed that Esteban was her boy; an easy mistake to make given that he clung to Edza as if she were his real mother, burying his head in her shawl and refusing to look at the men who had captured them.

This moved the Berber, who began to cry as he explained the situation. His only son, the light of his life and the hope of his old age, was being tortured in the sultan's notorious underground prison in Meknes. To secure the boy's release, he had been ordered to kidnap some important Spanish officials. He had succeeded in bribing the servants to abandon the place that afternoon, but had not calculated on their mistress being away from home. Despite the mix-up, he still felt he had no choice but to turn Edza and Esteban over to the sultan. Even if they were not infidels themselves, they belonged to a Spanish household. Surely kidnapping them would inspire terror in the invading Europeans? Perhaps it might even provide some sort of ransom, though undoubtedly nothing as generous as what might have been expected had they been more important people.

When he finished his explanation, Edza threw herself at his feet, praying to Allah for mercy. She had no care for herself, she said, but surely the Berber understood her fears for her only son, the light of her life and the hope of her old age. How could he condemn this innocent child to a life of slavery, torn from his mother's arms? Ultimately, the men were moved by Edza's piety to a compromise. They agreed to let her disguise Esteban as a girl so that he could stay with her in the harem to which she would doubtless also be confined. Moulay Ismail, prodigious in all his appetites, was famous for having more than five hundred concubines. Perhaps amidst such a crowd Edza and her child would not be noticed. Moreover, it was well known that the sultan's tastes ran more to European than to Moroccan women. He had even asked the French king, Louis XIV, for his daughter's hand in marriage. And though he had been refused, he continued to model both himself on the Sun King, and his spectacular palace of Meknes upon Versailles.

That was where the prisoners were headed: to the vast walled city the sultan was building with slave labour. According to the Berber, he worked them to death building his palaces, prisons, barracks, warehouses, stables, and aqueducts. It was claimed that when they grew weak, his slaves were beheaded by the sultan personally and mixed into the building materials on the spot, to reinforce the mortar with their blood and bones. The more Edza heard of the sultan's cruelty, the more willing she became to pretend Esteban was a girl and hide him in the harem. It took five days to reach Meknes by donkey cart; they had plenty of time to perfect his disguise. En route, the boy acquired a simple peasant dress, a shawl to cover his short hair, and dainty embroidered slippers, which he admired greatly. Edza outlined his eyes with kohl and, despite his protests, pierced his ears with a sharp needle and hung her own gold earrings in them. The earrings made all the difference. Wearing them, he became a very convincing girl.

The travellers smelled Meknes before they reached it, because of the sultan's habit of impaling the heads of his enemies on spikes topping the city walls. It was odd that someone so dedicated to sensual beauty could be so impervious to the stench of rotting flesh. The carpet-weaver, accustomed to the fresh air of the mountains, was disgusted, and stopped the donkey cart by a stream to pick some fragrant mint. Esteban clutched a few leaves to his nose and closed his eyes tight as they entered the main gate of the city, expecting to see signs of cruelty everywhere. But there was only the ordinary bustle of people on an ordinary day: barbers and shoemakers, fruit sellers and fishmongers, wandering scribes and musicians, and more donkeys, carts, camels, people, and buildings than he had ever seen before. Excited by the busy scene, he momentarily forgot that he had been kidnapped and was about to be sold into slavery.

After asking for directions from soldiers patrolling the crowds, the Berber led his prisoners down winding streets to a building guarded by yet more soldiers, with whom he conferred for a long time. They tied the cart to a gate where the exhausted donkey immediately fell into a profound meditation.

On foot they traversed a labyrinth of courtyards and tunnels and staircases, arriving at last at a grand hall where some very tall Africans in splendidly coloured robes were in conference. This was the infamous Black Guard, or "Abid," the best fighting force in North Africa. Originally slaves themselves, they were now among the most important people in the empire and entirely in the sultan's confidence. The commanding officer took one look at the three travellers, laughed a mirthless laugh, and slapped the carpet-weaver across the face. He fell to the ground and then lay full length, his clasped hands in prayer position above his turbaned head. In a voice barely above a whisper the poor man asked for forgiveness for his error and begged for the life of his beloved son. The abid merely laughed again, kicked him hard in the ribs, and sent him on his way like a beaten dog.

Edza entreated the abid to let her and her innocent daughter go, since he had clearly recognized that they were not the intended hostages. But he retorted that Meknes never released prisoners except to the grave. He did agree, however, not to separate her from the girl and sent them both off to the harem to await the sultan's pleasure. And that is where they stayed for more than a year, cloistered away from the world.

The boy's parents were making efforts to find him, but even had they succeeded in retracing his steps, the whole city was an armed fortress and there would have been no way of securing his release. Esteban himself was quite content. He missed his parents from time to time, but living among beautiful ladies was not bad. Living in the harem was not so different from the life he had led in Ceuta, busy all day with Edza, except that now he was forced to dress like a girl. His dangling robes frustrated any attempt at energetic play, and it was impossible to run in the dainty slippers of which he had been so proud.

Those shoes taught Esteban something interesting. Like many spoiled boys, he had dismissed girls as inferior because they were not as brave or strong as men, but now he realized that what renders them weak is custom, not nature. How could girls become strong when they were unable to move freely? When he begged Edza to let him resume masculine attire, she reminded him how dangerous such a transformation would be. But even she was forced to concede that he could not stay in the women's quarters forever. He was growing like a weed. Soon enough his shoulders would broaden and he would sprout down on his upper lip, and then someone would recognize that he was not the girl they had been calling "Aziza." Inevitably both of them would be punished; probably killed.

Using her only wealth — the gold earrings Esteban had been wearing — Edza was able to bribe a peddler who came to the harem every week with a cartload of fresh melons. He agreed to smuggle the boy out of the city with him and get him back to Ceuta. Edza cut off Esteban's hair, which had grown down to his shoulders, and outfitted him with boys' clothes which she had acquired. All the peddler had to do was carry the boy out of the harem in the large straw basket he wore strapped to his shoulders, and then off they went together, Esteban sitting boldly in his cart, an inconspicuous country lad, trotting through the city and home to freedom.

His parents had remained in the same house in Ceuta, hoping someday their only son would find his way home.

They were speechless with joy when he returned unharmed, and Esteban was ashamed to realize how little he had missed them. His mother insisted that they return to Spain immediately, where he would receive a proper education and take up manly pursuits — fencing and drinking and the practice of medicine.

∽

THE ROOM WAS HUSHED, the company lost in a collective dream of girls dressed as boys and boys dressed as girls, colourful pirates and remote tropical islands, golden carpets floating on blue tiles, a cruel sultan building a city of human bones and keeping hundreds of women in his harem, when Beauharnois's voice cut into the silence, declaring that Esther was not only a liar but an unimaginative one.

"This nonsense about an escape from the seraglio," he sneered. "Not only have we all heard this story — or one just like it — a thousand times before, it is not even about you."

"I enjoyed the girl's tales very much, Governor General," Madame Lévesque protested.

"Esther has done exactly what you asked of her, despite feeling ill," Hocquart added. "So I think it is time we took our leave."

"My, my, Hocquart. Apparently your inability to find yourself a wife has not kept you from becoming a doting father."

The two men stared at each other with frank hostility. Then Hocquart gestured to Esther, who stood up, curtsied to the assembly, and said to Beauharnois, "Thank you, Mon Seigneur, for a delicious dinner." Hocquart took her by the arm and led her out of the great room, down the hall past two bowing footmen, and into the sudden chill of the night and the dazzle of countless stars.

The pine-scented air was sharp and clean after the aromas of rich food and perfumed and pomaded dinner guests. Side by side they stood on the terrace, staring down at the quiet river rippling far below. Esther had never been to the top of Cap Diamant before and could only imagine the view when the sun was shining. It must go on forever. In the moonlight, the rigging of ships moored in the harbour trembled like spider webs. It seemed impossible that such dainty structures carried people and freight across the oceans of the world. A world made all the bigger and more mysterious by the stories she had been telling.

Fiddle music floated up from a party somewhere. They could also hear the barking of dogs, voices raised in anger, laughter, a baby crying. The busy world carried on, making them both feel lonely, suspended outside of ordinary life. Hocquart sighed, looking across the river to Lévis, where twinkling firelight suggested happy families warm and snug inside their houses. The lights of the village of Lorette still burned to the north. Turning, Hocquart let his eyes follow the course of the river down to Trois-Rivières and Montreal, cities he rarely visited but where Beauharnois went often for both work and pleasure.

"Why must he always insult me?" Hocquart murmured, more to himself than to his companion.

"He is jealous, Monsieur Hocquart," Esther replied, shivering a little, not unpleasantly, in the cold.

"Why? He has a title and crowds of followers. He has the ear of His Majesty and private audiences with Queen Marie."

"Nonetheless, you are happy and he is not."

"In what way do I seem happy?"

"You love your work and you enjoy your own company. Compared to you, the Governor General cares far too much about what others think of him. People like him can never be content."

"Like your stories, Esther, your interpretations of things around you may not always be true. But I do find them interesting."

And together they watched as a meteor streaked across the sky on a journey from an unknown origin to an unknown destination.

SEVEN

"El Dios es tadrozo mas no es olvidadozo."
(God may act slowly but He never forgets.)

AUTUMN'S GOLD WAS SOON spent. The days grew shorter and colder and the mood of the people grew more sombre. But to Marie-Thérèse's surprise, Esther relished the prospect of a hard winter. She said she had suffered greatly from the heat in Africa, being once so sunburned that she shed her skin like a snake, and therefore required the contrary experience of freezing in order to recalibrate her body temperature properly. She claimed that this was a well-known scientific fact; surely Marie-Thérèse knew that doctors habitually immersed fever patients in tubs of ice? Well then, it was for the same reason she needed to experience the terrors of frost in New France.

The housekeeper did not know what to make of the temperamental girl entrusted to her care. Often she seemed much older than her years, full of arcane information and impressive wisdom. But sometimes, in the midst of analyzing events around her with extraordinary acuity and even compassion, she would suddenly say something caustic, her lip curling with such glib condescension Marie-Thérèse felt like slapping her, or let fall a remark so funny that the housekeeper burst out laughing. Esther might act the part of a spoiled miss of the upper classes with no object in life but perpetual diversion, begging to go the market to buy trifles. Then again she might become profoundly sad, revealing the part of her that remained a lost child. Once only, seeing silent tears running down Esther's face and receiving nothing but a shake of the head when she inquired what was wrong, Marie-Thérèse had tried to comfort her, breaching the invisible barrier Esther erected around herself. The girl softened into her embrace, meeting Marie-Thérèse's inquiring gaze with eyes so anguished it was clear nothing would ever console her. Then she sobbed herself to sleep, rocking back and forth in the woman's arms in a trance of helpless misery.

Luckily these dark moods were infrequent, or Esther hid them well when they occurred. And she could usually be drawn out of introspection by a request for a story, of which she seemed to have an inexhaustible supply. This was good, because Marie-Thérèse had discovered in herself an equally inexhaustible love of listening. As the days grew shorter and colder, she drew Esther's tales around her for comfort. Through Esther's tales, her imagination was escorted to fantastic places she'd never been. She got to know characters who seemed more real to her than any of those around her: rich people who looked right through her and poor people working too hard to pass the time of day with her. She preferred the company of Esther and her phantoms.

Often the Intendant would contrive to be passing by during one of these storytelling sessions. He would peer into the kitchen or one of the storerooms — wherever Esther and Marie-Thérèse might be — on the pretext of looking for something, and then linger by the door, the object of his search forgotten, until one or the other of the women invited him to take a seat. He would appear momentarily nonplussed and then insist that he needed to take more notes. In his October 26 report to the Minister of the Marine he had begged the authorities "to prescribe me the direction of this girl," but of course it would be impossible to get any instructions from them until May or more likely June; no French navigator would brave the westward journey before then. Even if the Saint Lawrence were running freely, ice floes around the Newfoundland banks made sailing in the early spring far too treacherous. But what he expected, when that long-awaited letter finally came, was that he would be told to send Esther Brandeau packing at once — as he should have done the day she arrived. He had hesitated at the time because she was penniless and he was wary of setting a precedent. He was still concerned with that possibility, as he had no intention of paying for the passage of illegal immigrants in the future. She had caused him nothing but trouble since the day she arrived.

Esther would apologize profusely and thank him for his continued kindness to her; she might even offer to make him a cup of chocolate to drink while listening to her tale. Marie-Thérèse would scurry off to find him pen and paper for his "report" while he found somewhere comfortable to install himself. The whole production would become more formal and complicated with Hocquart in attendance. Esther knew that he frequently quizzed Marie-Thérèse in her absence as to whether the housekeeper had learned anything new about her.

When he was ready, Esther would close her eyes and fold her olive-skinned hands in her lap, seeming almost to fall into a dream. Her voice was melodious and faintly foreign; though her French was impeccable, there was something odd about it that no one yet had identified. Her "r's" rolled more richly, perhaps, her vowels were softer, her cadences more varied. Whatever it was, this exotic inflection was aptly suited to the stories she told, so often strange and hard to believe. Yet though small details might vary in the telling, the central facts remained the same, giving each episode of the unfolding saga not only credibility but, with Marie-Thérèse at least, canonical status.

Most often the housekeeper requested to hear stories about Joaquin, the ugly brute with the sensitive soul, and his unquenchable love for the poor slave girl, Aissata. Esther would retort that Monsieur Hocquart would not enjoy a silly romance intended for lovelorn ladies and besides, it was in no way relevant to his investigation. In its place, she would tell a nautical tale, detailing a trading expedition south from Spain to the Guinea coast or westbound to the sugar islands. But one day the Intendant grew curious, and insisted that he was the best judge of what was relevant, not her. So she relented.

~

AFTER JOAQUIN LEFT AISSATA he was sad for a very long time. He was sad during the revelry with the Portuguese militia; he was sad on the vessel that brought him back to Cadiz; he was sad in the oxcart that took him home to his village. In this sadness, all his thoughts were drawn inward. For many days he sat, unmoving, in his mother's house, while she wept and prayed for her poor injured child, relieved to have him home again but angry to find him broken both in body and in spirit. Later he went down to the docks to mend his brothers' nets and listen to the sea croon and cry, whisper and rant. He had become convinced that it was trying to talk to him, and that if he listened properly he would come to understand the meaning of his life. "Wish, wish," the waves chanted, flooding the shore. "See, see," they hissed, receding among the pebbles on the beach. "There is nothing I wish to see anymore but Aissata," Joaquin thought to himself. "But I do not deserve her, and my punishment is that I will never see anything again."

And then one day, while he was untangling an especially wicked snarl of rope, Joaquin heard a shriek and a splash as a child fell off the end of a pier. He'd been unaware of her presence until that moment, so focussed was he on his work. He called out loudly for help, sure that someone else must be near, but nobody responded. Meanwhile the splashing and screaming continued, punctuated with episodes of coughing as the victim inhaled salt water.

Joaquin panicked, listening to those frantic cries for help, before realizing that the fact that he couldn't see didn't mean he couldn't swim towards the child's voice and bring her to safety. He told her to keep calm; to move her legs and arms back and forth like scissors and to keep her head above the water. And then he jumped in. In a trice he had a pair of thin slippery arms around his neck and, swimming vigorously, enjoying the forgotten feeling of power in his thrashing legs, of capability in his strong arms, he brought the sobbing child to shore.

As she clung to him with her face tucked into his neck, her breath warm against his cold skin, something that had been frozen inside him for months thawed. He murmured words of encouragement to the girl, rocking her in his arms. Her name was Estella, and she explained that she hadn't learned to swim because she was lame in one leg. She asked him if he would teach her and he promised her that he would. They sat quietly for a moment on the rocky beach, glad to be alive.

Now other voices reached them: the girl's frantic mother and younger siblings; the butcher, wanting to be helpful; a couple of idle boys looking for excitement. When they realized what had happened, Joaquin became a hero. There was a big fiesta that night in his honour; the butcher roasted a suckling pig on a spit and the whole village celebrated. They rejoiced to see the blind boy drawn out of his misery, his face transformed from a marble mask crossed by a wicked red scar to the friendly open visage they remembered from his childhood.

Perhaps it was coincidence, but the very next morning

Joaquin opened his eyes to an impression of light, and within the week he could see again. His sight continued to improve over the following months. His mother attributed the miracle to her daily prayers to the Virgin Mary, the local doctor to time and the kindness of nature, but Joaquin himself was convinced that it was a sign of divine forgiveness. Though he had failed to rescue Aissata, he'd been able to save another girl in her place. Convinced it was his destiny, he married Estella and had three healthy children, though nothing could take the place of his first love, the sea, and he was away from his family more often than he was with them.

Monsieur Hocquart, do you remember the story I told at the Governor General's banquet about Joaquin, Doctor Esteban, and me when we were marooned on the island we named Tortugas? During our exile, we spoke frequently of the likelihood of our deaths, and of our remorse for our earthly transgressions, and we prayed for forgiveness from the merciful Lord above. Even in my childhood, when I had much less to regret than I do now, I often felt guilty and sad; however, my conscience weighed less heavily than those of my companions. Because they were older, and perhaps because they were men, life had offered them more opportunities for adventure and, correspondingly, for misadventure. Though I envied them their freedom, I recognized the heavy burden of responsibility that goes with it.

Oddly enough, the educated doctor and the illiterate sailor, so different in their looks, manners, and upbringing, had similar regrets. Both of them were tormented by the knowledge that they'd abandoned the women who had saved their lives.

So they made a solemn oath, pricking their thumbs with a knife and mingling their blood — a procedure which astonished me greatly, since they had scorned this ritual when they had witnessed it among the pirates — that if they survived, each would seek out his long-lost benefactor and rescue her if she were still alive.

Joaquin became obsessed with this promise. He called on Aissata in his sleep and sighed her name when he awoke. He swore to God that if he were allowed to escape this cursed rock, he would not rest until he brought her to freedom. At first I believed this obsession to be nothing more than the fermentation of guilt in a mind with nothing else to occupy it. All of us become vulnerable to such chimeras when we are ill, or anxious, or have gone astray in our lives, do we not? However, Joaquin remained determined to rescue Aissata even after we were safe aboard *Le Lys*. By contrast, Esteban abandoned his own vow immediately and proclaimed that once we were back on dry land he would stay there.

It turned out that the doctor was going home to be wed. His parents had picked out a girl for him a few short months before; it was in response to this engagement that he had run away to sea. At that time the prospect of marriage had seemed dull. He had hoped for one last adventure as a bachelor. Now, having had more adventure than he had anticipated, he craved nothing more than a hot meal and a soft bed. Esteban drew such amusing pictures for us of his future as a doddering greybeard, playing chess in the village square, that neither Joaquin nor I had the heart to reproach him for breaking his promise to rescue Edza from the sultan's harem; we were much too grateful at having been rescued ourselves to blame our friend for looking forward to a peaceful life.

But Joaquin did not falter in his own resolve. He asked the captain to let him disembark at the Cape Verde Islands and Pontevez agreed, though he thought it absurd that an old man so recently rescued from death should wish to be abandoned on an island teeming with savages. Obviously, since we were not French citizens, he had no obligation to bring us back with him; nonetheless Esteban and I were disappointed in this lack of official resistance. We pleaded with Joaquin to recover his strength before undertaking such a difficult quest. We also suggested, as gently as we could, that he might wish to say a proper goodbye to his wife and children, in case it didn't end well or took longer than anticipated. But nothing we said had any influence upon him. He was a man who had made an oath before God; a man whose magnetized heart pulled him in one direction and one direction only.

How he was going to find a single black slave in a country built on the backs of such people was a mystery, but he declared that his soul would not be at peace unless he made the attempt. Belonging nowhere and to no one, I offered to accompany him. To my chagrin, Joaquin insisted that I could only stay with him until *Le Lys* sailed, and then must leave with the other members of the crew. This quest belonged to him and him alone, he declared; moreover, as a white girl, I would certainly have a better future in Europe than in Africa.

Not yet accustomed to thinking of myself as either white or a girl, I was puzzled by this argument. I was also annoyed that he felt it was his duty to find a new chaperone for me, as though I weren't old enough to take care of myself. Esteban immediately offered to adopt me and bring me to Spain, but since he was giving up the seafaring life, his proposal wasn't appealing. Joaquin understood my reluctance to abandon the sea; he made Monsieur Fourget, who was a career sailor, promise to take me along with him on his future voyages. Then we all went ashore for a much-needed leave. To tell the truth, I was as excited as Joaquin himself at the prospect of finding the woman who had once saved his life.

Of course, for me it was no more than a game. I doubted that we could find someone Joaquin hadn't seen for forty years, but I was happy enough to accompany him. His quest gave shape to what might otherwise have been mere desultory wandering around in the heat of the day; I was given the opportunity to see a lot of faces and places while he asked if anyone knew where he could find Aissata, groping for words in the language he had not used for so long.

Miraculously, Joaquin remembered the names and relative ages of Aissata's family members; but, having been blind when he lived with them, he was unable to provide descriptions of anyone, even his beloved. Whenever he was asked what she looked like, he could only respond "an angel," which was not particularly useful for identifying a woman in her fifties who had undoubtedly lived a hard life, if she was still alive at all.

After four days, these interviews were growing tedious and even Joaquin was becoming discouraged. But suddenly someone called out to us that she knew the woman we were seeking. The voice came from a stall heaped with bananas, mangoes, papayas, tamarinds, and that curious tropical fruit called the custard apple, which tastes like aromatic soap. Behind the mountain of produce stood a tiny old lady, a lady so old that her eyes were lost in the folds of her papery skin and her chin bristled with stray white hairs. She was smoking a pipe, which made her speech even harder than usual to understand, but Joaquin understood that a woman named Aissata ran an inn called The Lost Boy on other end of the island, and that if we asked around the market we should be able to find a driver willing to take us there.

Luck was on our side. We found a ride that very afternoon. Before leaving, I conferred with Captain Pontevez who said that I could go wherever I pleased, but that he intended to set sail for France in four days with or without me. I promised to return in time, and then Joaquin and I set off across the island in a cart heavily laden with bolts of cloth. The driver told us these were used both as clothing and as currency on the islands, and were highly prized by African traders on the mainland, who were not able to purchase them. We didn't understand much of what he told us, but there was evidently some kind of illegal smuggling going on — and the proprietor of The Lost Boy was involved in it, for he was headed right to her place.

We slept overnight under the stars on a pile of the cloths and then resumed our journey early the next day. Both my companions were uncommunicative, so I spent my time listening to the birds and watching them swoop through the pale morning sky. The day was hot and still, the countryside as empty as if it had been the first morning of Creation. We stopped a couple of times to pick fruit from the trees and once to drink from a clear stream but I doubt if a dozen words passed between us during the whole trip.

At nightfall we pulled up to The Lost Boy. It was a small pink building glowing palely at the edge of a steep cliff overlooking the ocean. A wide porch ran around all four sides, surrounded by brilliant flowers and tall date palms heavy with fruit. I barely had time to take in the beauty of the setting before the driver grunted that he needed us to help him unload his cargo. As I was helping him, I heard a sudden intake of breath and felt Joaquin leave my side. I looked up and saw the silhouette of a graceful woman framed by the door of the house, her face in darkness. He sang her name as though it were a hymn and she ran down the stairs into his arms.

I stayed with them overnight and was privileged to hear her story — or at least as much of it as Joaquin was able or willing to translate. This much I gleaned.

After Aissata was captured, she was sold to a rich merchant to assist his cook in the kitchen and to help serve meals when he had guests, which was a frequent occurrence. One day, when she was serving dinner to a group of his business associates, she caught the eye of an elderly Jewish trader. He offered to buy her for a good price, being in need of a housekeeper. Her employer, who had plenty of other slaves, agreed. Aissata was distraught. She felt safe where she was, and as long as she stayed there she could see her family from time to time. But slaves had no rights, so despite her pleas for mercy she was sent off with her new owner. He was kind enough to let her say goodbye to her mother before they set sail, which reassured her, but of all the many hardships she had undergone, leaving Cape Verde was the hardest yet.

Life with the trader, whose name was Jacobo Farrega, was good. He was kind, gentle, and appreciative of all she did. He even called her "Miss Aissata," and said "please" and "thank you" to her, which no white person had ever done before. His own family had been forced to flee Portugal to escape the Inquisition so that, like her, he had been forced to start over in a new place. What he told her about the history of the Jews — perpetually fleeing slavery and torture, living in exile among strangers, the subject of their contempt and mistrust — made her feel a kind of kinship with him. In time, this deepened to affection. When ultimately he proposed marriage to her, she accepted, even though he was much older. They were rewarded with the birth of one son, Benjamin, who was now grown up with a family of his own.

Jacobo's business had been selling Cape Verdean cloth to other European merchants. Although the Portuguese Crown had prohibited this trade, the Jews operated outside the law, which caused antagonism between them and other Portuguese merchants. In the past this rivalry had occasionally led to violence, including the Inquisition itself coming to Cape Verde, but things had been peaceful for some time. One night, however, their warehouse was mysteriously set ablaze and her husband died, foolishly running into the flames to rescue his stock. Aissata, not sure who their enemies were or whether they would strike again, returned to Cape Verde with a small capital and Benjamin, at that time a boy of seven. There she had discovered that her family had died of starvation during a terrible drought and that she and her son were alone in the world. But they were free and had money, so she decided to start over, buying a small inn at the far end of the island. She continued her husband's trade. Fishermen would come ashore, ostensibly to sell their catch, and leave with cloth that they could resell to traders along the coast.

Joaquin said he was amazed at how well things had turned out for her. He had hardly dared hope to find her, much less find her free and healthy with property of her own. Now he could die in peace. She only stared at him with a sad smile on her face before replying that her life was not as good as he made it sound, because she was all alone in the world.

"What about your son?" he asked. "Is he the Lost Boy after whom you named the inn?"

"No, dear Joaquin," she replied. "That was you. It has always been you."

Hearing that, he took her in his arms. I crept from the room, to sleep under the stars and wonder at the mystery of our lives. The next morning I bid farewell to my friend Joaquin forever, and returned to my ship.

∼

BECAUSE HER EYES WERE closed, as they always were when she told her tales, Esther did not realize that Monsieur Hocquart had become more and more agitated as the romance of Joaquin and Aissata reached what she intended to be a happy ending. Certainly Marie-Thérèse had always been delighted with its resolution. It was only when the Intendant collapsed in a fit of coughing that she realized he was upset. She opened her eyes, bewildered, to watch as Marie-Thérèse ran to get him a glass of water. What was wrong now?

"You promote this character as a hero, yet he left his wife and children to take up with a criminal," Hocquart sputtered, when he regained his breath.

"Why is being a slave a crime, Monsieur Hocquart?" Esther asked. Slavery existed in New France; indeed, she'd heard that the Marquis de La Boische had twenty-seven slaves — a fact which seemed to justify her instinctive aversion to him — but the Intendant himself had always seemed both kind and rational. How could someone like him justify one human being claiming ownership of another?

"I am referring to Aissata's profession as a smuggler. Besides which, adultery is a sin."

"Surely on his part more than hers?" Esther persisted.

Hocquart, about to respond, decided that it was beneath his dignity to engage in discussions on the nature of morality with a young woman who was, nominally at least, his prisoner. "Go to your room at once, Esther. From now on you will stay there and stop wasting my housekeeper's time with this nonsense."

"But Monsieur Hocquart, please, I need her to help me with the baking. Don't forget Christmas is coming," Marie-Thérèse said, confronting her employer with uncharacteristic boldness.

When he saw the misery on both women's faces he added, "Fine, you may continue to help out in the kitchen, as needed. But no more storytelling."

"May I still use the library, Monsieur?" Esther whispered, almost afraid to ask.

"If you behave yourself."

With that, he turned his back and marched away, satisfied with the firm authority he had conveyed, though as unsure as ever what to do about his unpredictable charge. Young women never sailed unaccompanied to New France unless they had prospective husbands or employers or at least some local family waiting for them, but Esther Brandeau had no one to take her in. Although she claimed to be willing to work for whoever would have her, he did not feel it was prudent. Her identity could not be confirmed; how could he impose such a vagabond on anyone? It was his job to maintain the safety and security of the colony.

It didn't seem right, however, to throw the girl in prison for running away to sea. True, she had broken two laws by hiding her identity and dressing in masculine attire. But since she had hurt no one by doing either, he was not inclined to insist on punishment, no matter how offended Beauharnois might be. In fact, that the Marquis Charles Beauharnois de La Boische was offended made Intendant Gilles Hocquart all the more disposed to leniency.

Whenever he began to think about Esther his head hurt. Whenever she saw him slumped over with his head in his hands, she offered to make him a cup of chocolate. It was absurd how susceptible he was to Esther's chocolate — and to her tales. Both these enticements made him happy, and being happy made him lazy. He found excuses to listen to her like some slack-jawed habitant when he should be administering justice, running his shipbuilding operation, seeing to the countless tasks required to ensure the prosperity of the colony.

The girl's presence was a distraction; her tales a constant temptation.

Far worse than the seduction of the stories themselves was how they challenged his convictions. If he accepted what Esther said as true, his beliefs about the world would be put in doubt. In her version of reality slaves deserved freedom, infidels were as good as Christians, and women became the equals of men. Hocquart had read his Bible and he knew that the meek were destined to inherit the earth. But only at the Second Coming, not now! Esther Brandeau's radicalism had no place in this remote outpost of the empire of His Majesty King Louis XV.

EIGHT

"Mas vale cien años en cadena que
un año debaxo de la tierra."
(Better a hundred years of captivity than one year in the grave.)

BITTER NOVEMBER WINDS CLAWED the few remaining leaves from the trees to be churned into mud by the traffic of men and horses. The mud itself froze and thawed, froze and thawed, as the temperature dropped each night and rose, feebly, by noon. A simple walk to the market became both treacherous and filthy. It grew dark earlier and earlier, and the increasing gloom affected the mood of the town. Marie-Thérèse, deprived of Esther's stories, turned to housekeeping with a vengeance, yelling at the maids to sweep the invasive dirt from the house, wash the windows and beat the carpets. Though she had never been idle, she now found more work than ever to occupy her.

Not wanting to cause trouble for the housekeeper, Esther kept her distance. Draped in a heavy shawl, she passed the time reading in Hocquart's library, empty during the workday, and then retreated to her attic room at night when he wanted to use it himself. Outside the library window she could see people bundled up in thick woollen coats and bright red or blue toques, their horses' breath turning white as it steamed from their nostrils. Only the pine trees remained unchanged, as green and glossy as ever, revealing their true strength as their weaker cousins stood shivering and naked. Standing tall and dark at the edge of the Intendant's compound, they were the true natives of this place; they and the Indians.

Sometimes, in spite of Marie-Thérèse's fears about them, she imagined running away to join the Indians. Among them she could learn to paddle a birchbark canoe and hunt game-birds with a bow and arrow, then cook what she had killed over an open fire. Wearing comfortable clothes she could explore the wilderness freely. Sleeping in a wooden longhouse with a large noisy group would be as comforting and communal as bedding down on board ship, without the disadvantage of being wakened every four hours by the changing of the watch. The fantasy of becoming a noble savage became more and more appealing as her days of solitude stretched into weeks, and Esther decided to profit from her enforced isolation by learning more about the Indians.

The Intendant's library contained *The Jesuit Relations* in both Latin and French, so first she explored that strange encyclopaedia of bravery and horror, Huron customs and European voyages. She had encountered the works of Samuel de Champlain before but returned to them with new curiosity, more interested now in his accounts of Native life than his seafaring accomplishments. Her greatest discoveries, however, were Joseph Le Caron's dictionary of the Huron language and the phrasebook of Recollect Brother Gabriel Sagard. Having little else with which to occupy her days, and always having been fond of languages and quick to acquire them, she set out to study that of the aboriginals.

Esther's father had been a great believer in education; he had made sure even his daughters could read, write, and do basic arithmetic. These accomplishments behind her, the greatest pleasure of her childhood had been to sit in on her older brothers' tutorials in more advanced subjects such as philosophy, geometry, Latin, and Greek. From those experiences she knew it was best to copy out lists of foreign words in order to memorize them. Paper was hard to come by, but she managed to beg some from Marie-Thérèse, who foraged for scraps from Monsieur Hocquart's study and the courthouse. Day after day Esther worked away in private, waiting for an opportunity to impress the Intendant with her new knowledge. She hoped that given his great responsibility in the colony, Monsieur Hocquart would appreciate her diligence in acquiring the Huron dialect. Surely such commitment on her part would induce him to allow her to stay? But though he would look in on her occasionally, sometimes watching her silently from the doorway with his kind eyes, Hocquart no longer engaged her much in conversation. Once he said ominously, "Varin has news. We shall be seeing him soon. Prepare yourself." But Varin did not come, though Esther would have welcomed the challenge of his insolent interrogation, so lonely had she become.

She had spent most of her childhood like this: shuttling between the kitchen and the library searching for clues as to how to behave, learning to cook so that she could please people who were suspicious of her. Turning salty tears into sweet desserts as though such alchemy might transform who she was into something acceptable. How could her bold adventure, going to sea in boy's clothes, have led back to the same way of life as the one she had left?

But life was unfair; if Esther knew anything, she knew that. One of her earliest revelations had been the profound injustice of society, blaming or rewarding people for things over which they had absolutely no control or for which they could take no credit. In her own head she had continually asked questions she could not speak aloud, such as why men were considered superior to women. Now she found herself wondering why the Marquis de La Boische was held to be better than others because of his title. What was a marquis anyway? She didn't know, and suspected that few people did. But they accepted the convention that because he was a member of the aristocracy he ought to be revered, despite the fact that he was a horrible person and no one actually liked him.

And then, one morning, Esther woke to a world of white. Each window was garlanded with fragile flowers of ice. The trees, lately bare, were piled with snow as soft as eiderdown. A mad gaiety invaded Upper Town. All the ladies were clad in wonderful furs, their cheeks rosier from the slap of the cold than they'd ever been under a layer of rouge, as they went from house to house for evenings of cards and chess and music and dancing. Even the industrious habitants shared this festive mood. Winter was a time for revelry; people visited each other more often with the excuse that the weather made it impossible for them to pursue their proper trades. In some cases this was true, but even when it was not, most people got caught up in the prevailing mood of indulgence.

Except for Hocquart. His job had never been seasonal nor his character frivolous, and the burden of managing Esther had become increasingly problematic. She had been more or less under house arrest for the last month, but he was well aware that he should have sent her back to France while that was still possible. Rumours had reached him from Montreal, where Beauharnois was spending the winter, that the Governor General had taken to calling Esther "Hocquart's feral child," and making jokes at his expense, some of them quite improper.

Something had to change.

Meanwhile the gentry, perpetually on the lookout for a new source of diversion, kept demanding the girl's company to go skating on the sparkling river or to visit the Hurons at the village of Jeune Lorette. Those who had not been to Beauharnois's banquet wanted their turn in the audience; those who had already enjoyed the pleasure of her tale-telling wished for a repeat performance. Hocquart intended to quash all invitations but ultimately gave in to the request of Madame Lévesque, issued at a New Year's celebration at her own home. The stout and jolly chatelaine Esther had met at Beauharnois's dinner party was a member of one of the most powerful families in the colony, as well as a personal friend and ally.

Hocquart had few enough of those and no intention of alienating her, so he relented.

Early in January, on a day of dazzling sunlight, Madame Lévesque commandeered Esther for a day of sightseeing. She was accompanied by an elderly woman whose mild eyes peered out from a face deeply latticed with wrinkles. The two ladies, in their winter coats and voluminous shawls, were bundled under thick bearskins; squeezed in beside them, Esther could hardly breathe. The bearskins smelled at once rank and dusty, a blend of wet dog and old carpet. But the jingling of sleigh bells on the horses' collars was so gay, and the ice-covered branches overhead shone so brilliantly against the bright blue sky, and the opportunity to leave the smoky gloom of Hocquart's palace was so very welcome, that she overcame her distaste, and found herself stroking the rough black fur with a curious kind of pleasure.

"Where are we going, Madame Lévesque?" she asked.

"It is a surprise."

And with that, her hostess laid a gloved finger across her lips to indicate silence, before reaching under her furs to produce a bottle of cognac from which she poured each of her guests a warming sip. Her friend, whom she introduced as Madame Duplessis, demurred at first, but was persuaded that on such a cold day, liquor served a purely medicinal purpose.

"Madame Duplessis is very abstemious. She intended to take orders in her youth," Madame Lévesque explained.

"Why?" asked Esther, with such wide-eyed simplicity that Madame Duplessis was not offended, as ordinarily she would have been, but instead found herself trying to explain something too close to her heart for the superficiality of casual conversation.

"What other course is there for an intelligent woman?" she asked.

Esther was surprised by the old lady's sincerity. She herself had grown up fearing nuns, crossing the street when she saw them coming in order to avoid the evil eye. It had never occurred to her that a community of religious women might provide sanctuary rather than punishment.

"And yet you left the convent."

"Papa insisted on my marrying."

"Couldn't you resist?"

"What power does a sixteen-year-old girl have?"

"The power to run away."

"Like you?" Madame Duplessis laughed for the first time, showing a mouthful of surprisingly small and even white teeth. "No, my dear; I was never much of a rebel." And with that, she lapsed into a private meditation, signalling that the conversation was over. Her eyes closed and, without warning, the old lady gave a sigh and fell asleep, her head dropping onto Esther's shoulder as trustingly as that of a child.

"Let her rest, poor thing," said Madame Levesque. "She has been quite ill, which is why I invited her on this outing."

Esther tried not to move so that the old lady could sleep peacefully, awkward as it was to sit still as the *cariole* skidded, hitting a patch of ice, or jolted, becoming stuck in a rut so that the driver had to get down and push. She wondered at the trust shown to her by these strange women, and her own instinctive trust of them. Where were they taking her, and why had Hocquart suddenly allowed her to go? It was all very mysterious, but welcome nonetheless. Life had been so dull recently. Everyone else in the Intendant's household had been in a flurry of excitement about the celebration of Christmas and the prospect of time off to see family and friends. Esther had enjoyed more of Marie-Thérèse's companionship in the kitchen, but otherwise her life continued lonely and anxious.

They took the King's Road north from the city, passing many happy travellers on the way and witnessing others galloping their horse-drawn sleds perilously at the edge of the river ice. Madame Lévesque whispered to Esther that this favourite pastime of reckless boys during the long Quebec winter sometimes ended in tragedy. But there was no way of stopping it; even her own son, Joseph, now living in Montreal, refused to listen to reason and raced against his friends.

The road continued beside the river. Clustered along its edges were the whitewashed houses of the habitants, here and there interrupted by the larger stone mansions of the seigneurs whose land they worked. Madame Lévesque seemed to know the history of each estate they passed and gossip about all the families. In this way the ride passed quickly, until suddenly the carriage stopped and she announced, "We're here."

Esther looked up. Two Huron men stood under a nearby pine tree, regarding them with mild curiosity. They were both tall and dark, wearing deerskin coats decorated with ornate quillwork and hung about with embroidered pouches. Their deerskin trousers were gartered with embroidered bands and tucked into embroidered boots, and their long gleaming black hair was dressed in coiffeurs so fantastic they put the ladies at the Governor General's ball to shame. If these were their everyday clothes, Esther could not imagine how such splendid fellows would dress on festive occasions.

She was excited. This was the closest she'd been to a Native except at the market, where Marie-Thérèse would not allow her to approach even the smiling women and children. Away from the over-protective housekeeper for the first time, Esther was determined to say hello, trying out the vocabulary she had studied alone in Hocquart's library.

"*Kweh,*" she said, raising her palm in greeting. The men stared back at her, though one of them appeared to frown less than before. Seeing how little her enthusiastic welcome impressed them, Esther was mortified. Her dream of living free in the forest like an Indian maiden was suddenly revealed for the daydream it was; the silly fantasy of a silly girl with no power and no resources. Why had she allowed herself to be deluded? There was no escape for her, not in the forest, nor anywhere else. She didn't belong here, where families like Madame Lévesque's already went back three generations and the Natives had lived forever. She didn't belong anywhere, and never would.

She covered both eyes with her hands in an instinctive gesture of grief.

"No, no, you must look over there, Esther," said Madame Lévesque, puzzled, pointing to something in the distance. It shimmered and tumbled from a vast height in sparkling rivulets that reflected more light than a thousand chandeliers. It resembled glass but was alive; flowed like water yet was more composed. At its base frothed and billowed an apparently different substance, milky and opaque, turbulent and calm at the same time, as though waves had begun tumbling towards shore without arriving there to break on the vast white sands that stretched in all directions. Sands upon which dozens of people gathered in horse-drawn sleds and on foot, while dogs cavorted, barking and yipping, and more Indians stood silently watching, some wrapped in red and black blankets, others in leather garments pulling toboggans of provisions behind them.

What she beheld was a huge cataract, frozen mid-fall from almost a hundred feet high, retaining the memory of motion but suspended as though time itself had paused between breaths to admire it more fully.

"Where are we?" Esther whispered.

"The falls of Montmorency," Madame Lévesque replied.

Esther quickly clambered out of the *cariole*, not waiting for the other ladies to disengage themselves from their heavy layers of insulation. They in turn were quite content to admire the view from the comfort of their vehicle, and to enjoy her excitement vicariously. She ran towards the waterfall, quickly sinking into the snow up to her knees until she could run no further. The air was so pure she felt drunk, so cold her breath sparked in her lungs and caught in her chest in painful gasps.

Esther had had little experience of snow before this winter in Quebec, and none at all of snow this deep, as deep as a pond. At first she pretended to swim through it, making the ladies in the carriage laugh. Then she swung her arms across the peaks of the drifts so that a storm of white flakes whirled around her. Snow was such a strange substance, impossible to describe. It covered the ground like sand, as though it were quite dry and substantial. But as soon as it was touched, it magically dissolved. It floated down as delicate blossoms, spun webs as fine as lace, then gathered together in great clumps like sticky clay. When it froze it became transparent; otherwise it was opaque. Snow reminded her of many things that it was not, but all comparisons cancelled each other out so that it remained utterly and only itself.

She let herself fall onto her back and gazed up into the sky, the same blue dome that covered the earth. Where did it end? And, if it did end, what was beyond it? Crossing the ocean, Esther had often stared into the heavens feeling exactly like this: simultaneously small and infinite, enthralled by the paradox. In such a grand cosmos she herself was of no consequence, which was humbling. But at the same time it was liberating, because neither was anyone else. No matter how important they thought they were, they were lost among all the living and all the dead, in a world beyond their comprehension. The heavens do indeed declare the glory of God. But they also insist that everyone is equal.

Preoccupied with avoiding controversy and pleasing people since her masquerade had been discovered, Esther had forgotten this fleeting but all-encompassing revelation. Now it flooded back, accompanied by a supernatural fineness of discrimination that had her feeling the weight of each flake that tickled her eyelashes, hearing each sigh of the snow beneath her as it shifted under her weight, seeing innumerable gradations of blue in the sky above her and a thousand shifting forms in the clouds streaming unimaginably far overhead. She didn't need to become an Indian to worship nature.

It belonged to her as much — and as little — as it did to them.

"She is quite a discovery, this wild child of yours," Madame Duplessis remarked, watching Esther's rapture with a wistful smile on her face.

"I know. But I feel sorry for her; Hocquart has no idea what to do with her so she spends entire days all by herself in his library."

"Perhaps one of us might take her in."

"You should ask the Intendant to let her be your companion, Madeleine. Your eyes are so bad now. She could read to you."

"Do you think Monsieur Hocquart would agree to such a plan?" asked Madame Duplessis.

"I intend to insist he does," said Madame Lévesque.

Esther swam her way back to the carriage and climbed up to join them, covered with snow but happier than she'd been in months. She thanked the ladies for bringing her to this temple of beauty and agreed, reluctantly, that she'd experienced enough of it for one day. With a flick of the reins, they were off again.

Esther — who'd had little opportunity for exercise in her months of confinement and was exhausted in both body and mind — relaxed into the rhythm of the ride and the warmth of the bearskins. Now she was the one who felt sleepy. The ladies chatted about their health, their grandchildren, whether Esther was comfortable living with the Intendant, whether she was happy in New France, but were often quiet themselves as well. The falling snow seemed to insist upon silence, muffling the sound of the horses' hooves and the squeaking of the carriage; making their voices sound as hushed as if they were in a house of worship. As they drew closer to town, everyday sounds were subdued, the barking of a dog as startling as the red blanket of a passing Indian in that world of white.

And then the sled slowed, and stopped, and the tired horses tossed their snowy manes with a crystalline jingle of bells. They had arrived at the Intendant's palace. Esther scrutinized the long, two-storey stone building that had been her home for more than three months. When she arrived she had thought it spacious and elegant, but how grim and confining it looked after the fairyland of Montmorency Falls. It was easy to remember that laws were made in this building: laws to control the actions of New France and to punish those who failed to submit their will to that of the King and his representatives. Thus far she had succeeded in evading those laws because she was an outsider; no one knew how to apply conventional rules to her maverick behaviour. But the longer she stayed, the more difficult it would become to escape their confines. She would have to figure out some strategy to stay in New France without submitting.

Unsure what her next move ought to be, she did the only thing that came to mind. She jumped out of the carriage once more into the snow.

"You are as silly as a puppy his first winter, Esther," said Madame Lévesque, as she pounded the brass *fleur-de-lys* knocker on the huge oak door. "Go get out of those wet clothes right away while we speak to Monsieur Hocquart."

As soon as Marie-Thérèse appeared, the ladies asked to see the Intendant. They were ushered into a cold, damp waiting room while Esther ran down the hall, leaving puddles as she went. Madame Duplessis lowered herself gingerly into a deep armchair decorated with a needlepoint picture of nymphs in gauzy white garments dancing between marble fountains and green trees covered with ripe lemons shining like miniature suns — an image from a world an ocean away: a world she herself had never visited. Madame Lévesque looked about for cushions and a footstool to prop up the old lady's swollen feet. She was able to wrap her friend in a blanket of coarse local wool, then settled herself close to the fire, which she stirred up with a poker held between stiff fingers.

When Monsieur Hocquart arrived a half-hour later, bewildered at the summons but unwilling to turn away such prominent citizens, he found the two ladies as comfortably ensconced in his parlour as though they were in their own homes, drinking chocolate prepared for them by Esther and biscuits baked by Marie-Thérèse. They hadn't waited for him to offer hospitality but commandeered it themselves, and continued to act as though they were in charge, sending his servants away and asking him to sit down and listen to what they had to say.

The Intendant perched, reluctantly, on the edge of a hard wooden chair — rough pine, of local manufacture — as though about to spring up any minute. He did not appreciate having his workday interrupted. But he listened to Madame Lévesque's proposal with increasing interest; perhaps this really would be the best course for everyone involved. The girl would be taken care of until orders arrived in the spring, and he himself would cease to be the subject of trivial gossip and speculation amongst the idle rich. No longer would conversations stop abruptly when he entered a room, nor would the

Governor General make scurrilous jokes at his expense. He would perform a service to Madame Duplessis and help himself at the same time.

He agreed to let Esther go with her.

Marie-Thérèse was heartbroken; she couldn't imagine returning to her former solitude. She asked timidly if the girl might stay longer, perhaps until after Easter with all its attendant festivities, but Hocquart fixed her with a stern look and told Esther to go get her things and to be grateful for finding so benevolent a patron. The housekeeper accompanied Esther to her room, where she gave her a fierce hug and whispered "You are the daughter I never had." Esther hugged her back for the first and only time, and pressed into the older woman's hand the wooden *moussoir* she had brought all the way from France: the only thing of value she owned.

"You will need this to make Monsieur Hocquart his chocolate," she said, between laughter and tears. And then she picked up her bag and walked out of the Intendant's palace into a new life.

NINE

"Aboltar cazal, aboltar mazal."
(A change of scene, a change of fortune.)

ALTHOUGH MADAME DUPLESSIS SPENT her early years on her father's seigneury in the Sillery district and her adolescence at the Ursuline convent, after marriage she resided in a big stone house on the Chemin Saint-Louis. It was a very grand building indeed, two storeys high like many residences in upper town but differing from most in having extensive land behind it. Since the death of her husband, she had ceded the house to her oldest son and his family and moved into a much smaller building adjacent, though she spent as much time as possible in her old garden. She loved the modest dower house of her widowhood where everything she needed was on the ground floor: her bedroom, her chapel, the kitchen, dining room, and parlour. Upstairs were the servants' quarters, at the moment almost empty as the housekeeper lived out, as did the father and son who took care of her horse and carriage. The cook had her own room, where she kept an overfed cat that spent most of the day drowsing by the kitchen hearth; another room housed a painfully shy maid named Claire. Would Esther mind sharing with her?

Briefly, Esther missed her closet at Hocquart's; she was both unused to intimacy and fearful of giving away any of her secrets in an unguarded moment. But as soon as she met Claire her fears were allayed: the girl was so small that she took up almost no space and so timid that she made no demands. A wall-eyed orphan from Dieppe, Claire had made the trip to New France with her brother Philippe, both of them having signed three-year terms as indentured servants. Philippe, whom she idolized, had since moved to Trois-Rivières with his employer. Claire missed him dreadfully.

It took Esther nearly a week to get this much information out of her chamber-mate and it was another week before the poor girl got up the nerve to ask her anything in return. Claire asked shyly if the story she'd heard was true. Had Esther really been brought up by apes? Esther simply laughed, and replied that every tale was about its teller. Claire puzzled over this response for a few minutes before inquiring how Esther had learned to speak French, and wear clothes, and eat with a knife and fork, since animals did none of those things.

Esther could not bring herself to embroider her tales too elaborately for someone so innocent, so she told the girl that she had later been adopted by a woman, who treated her badly. Was no one kind to her? Claire asked, almost in tears. Yes, Esther hastened to assure her; one of the woman's sons, a boy named Daniel, had been a good and loving friend. But he had gone away to sea and she had missed him so much that she had disguised herself as a boy in order to follow him to New France, the same way Claire had followed her own brother; however, it appeared Daniel was not here. So, again like Claire, Esther was all alone in the world.

From this moment on, Claire was as devoted to Esther as if they were flesh and blood. Nor was the friendship one-sided; there was plenty Esther could learn from a girl her own age who had been in New France two years longer than she had. The most important of these skills was skating, the favourite winter sport of the locals, at which Claire had become very adept. They were permitted to enjoy this activity every Sunday after church when the entire town turned out, gaily apparelled, upon the frozen river. Esther was dubious, but after Claire managed to procure an extra set of blades she was persuaded to go.

Against the cobalt sky, the river was a tumble of diamonds. It shone with an almost painful radiance, reflecting nothing, self-contained, cold-hearted and unknowable as the new land itself. Skaters moved across its surface tentatively at first, unsure of their footing, then with increasing confidence as the ice held firm under their weight. Spreading their arms wide for balance, scissoring their legs, they flew faster and faster, hooting with pleasure. Some formed long lines, "cracking the whip," snapping off the unlucky person at the end of the queue across the ice. Couples danced to their own private music.

Children fell, and howled, and picked themselves up, and fell again.

One tall plain nun maintained her dignity in this rowdy company, gliding along without apparent effort, her legs invisible under the voluminous folds of her habit. With her arms swinging back and forth in billowing sleeves, she resembled an enormous black and white bird, at once predatory and serene. Claire identified her as Mother Claude, superior of the Hôpital Général of Quebec. Compared to her, Esther was awkward as a fledgling newly tumbled from the nest. Her centre of gravity seemed displaced, her limbs dangled uselessly from her insubstantial spine, and each breath stabbed as though the air was lanced with tiny shards of glass. For the first time since she arrived in New France, Esther understood why people feared the cold. Her bones ached with the knowledge that the cold could kill her. It could kill her incidentally, without a backward glance, because her pounding heart and hot breath disturbed its silent architecture. Because blood was red and frost was white.

Still, she determined to make the most of this ephemeral freedom and pushed off vigorously from one foot to the other, trying to step and glide, step and glide, just as Claire instructed. Much to her chagrin, she found herself suddenly flat on her back, looking into Mother Claude's amused face. She took the nun's offered hand for support and heaved herself up. Mother Claude simply smiled, nodded, and skated away, spraying her with a froth of shaved ice in the process.

Esther tried skating for a few more minutes with Claire's encouragement, but soon had to give up. Her feet were on fire. She hobbled to the edge of the river and sat down heavily on a rude bench of split timbers. With frost-stiffened fingers, she pulled off her skates, almost weeping from the pain in her toes. Who needed martyrdom when skating was available? How could people insist that this was fun? But around her the revelry continued, innocent and bright as the hand-knitted toques and mittens the children wore, the colourful blankets of the few Hurons observing them with amusement from the safety of the shore.

When they returned from this first outing, Esther told Madame Duplessis of her surprise at seeing a nun skating. She had always thought nuns too solemn and self-important to engage in frivolous amusements. Her employer replied that Mother Claude was so important that she could do whatever she wished. A daughter of the former governor of Montreal, the mother superior derived from a family of aristocratic soldiers from whom she had inherited her upright carriage and air of unshakeable authority. Like her sister Louise, who ran a successful lumbering operation, she was famous for her keen business sense. She was also renowned for her hospitality, lavishing banquets on all visiting nobles in the hopes of their patronage. No one who came to the city left without paying their respects to her; no one went away hungry or unimpressed. Not for the first time, Esther reflected that women had more independence in the New France than they did in the old, and could rise to higher positions of authority. She was glad her travels had ended here, and guardedly hopeful for her own prospects.

Over time, Esther grew more comfortable on skates, though she had plenty of bruises to testify to the hazards of the learning process. The prospect of an hour of freedom flying along the river made the tedium of sitting through Mass almost worthwhile. Hocquart had not compelled her to attend services with his household, but now she was required to pray two or three times a day in Madame Duplessis's private chapel, as well as to attend Mass with her employer at Notre-Dame-de-la-Paix every Sunday. She had been to the big cathedral before, with Marie-Thérèse, but on those occasions she had studied the congregation rather than paying attention to what the priest was saying. Now that she spent so many hours each day reading devotional literature, she was familiar with the liturgy and could mouth the Latin words with the other congregants, though little of it impressed her sceptical soul.

She was fascinated by Madame Duplessis's favourite book, *The Life of the Venerable Mother Marie de l'Incarnation*, by her son Claude Martin, all seven hundred and fifty-seven pages of which she read aloud when not stopped by her employer to analyze and discuss parts of the text. Madame Duplessis nodded her head emphatically when Marie confessed her preference for the serenity of life in the monastery at Tours as compared to the "commotion" of family life. She told Esther how bitterly she herself had wept when compelled to give up her dream of the cloisters and how much, as a young wife and mother, she had missed having time to study, think, and pray; how she'd only recovered her former tranquillity of spirit in old age and widowhood.

For her part, Esther was moved to tears when she read, in one of Marie's letters to her son, that her compulsion to abandon him in order to follow her religious vocation made her "the most cruel of all mothers." And they were both transported by Marie's observation in another letter that "We see nothing, we walk gropingly, and … ordinary things do not come about as they have been foreseen and advised. One falls and, just when one thinks oneself at the bottom of an abyss, one finds oneself on one's feet."

After they had worked their way through this volume, Esther made bold to suggest that they read her own favourite, a novel by a devout Englishman she had noticed in Monsieur Hocquart's library. Madame Duplessis immediately arranged to borrow *Robinson Crusoe* from the Intendant, who was amused to hear that Esther had proposed reading something like that to the old lady.

Madame Duplessis adored the book, as Esther anticipated that she would, despite her general preference for tracts and saints' lives. She was particularly partial to Crusoe's rescue of the man he called Friday, and the mutual love between the two. She said that the castaway Englishman's spiritual tutelage of the gentle savage was remarkably similar to Marie de l'Incarnation's relationship to her own Indian girls; though Defoe was, sadly, a Protestant, he seemed to have genuine insight into the necessity for absolute trust in the Lord. Esther admitted that she herself was principally fascinated by Crusoe's resourcefulness all the years he lived alone on the island, building two homes, growing corn and rice, taming goats, learning to make cheese and bread and even his own clothes. For her he was not a wicked man brought to perfect faith but instead a good example of the truth illustrated by La Fontaine in his fables that "God helps those who help themselves."

∾

WHILE ESTHER BRANDEAU AND Madeleine Duplessis had been travelling the world through books, the real world outside was waking up. Each tree in Madame's old garden began to burst with buds the yellow-green of distilled sunlight. From minute to minute fresh life appeared. The very air shimmered as though it too had been frozen solid like the river. Released from bondage, it rippled and flexed glad muscles just as Esther did, running outside to examine the new foliage.

That bush that had flaunted brilliant red branches all winter against the snow — what was it? And the nondescript thing with impatient golden flowers that came before its leaves, and those tiny white blossoms that popped up here and there between rocks and even under the snow, thriving in the hardest conditions. Did they have the same flowers in France? She had paid scant attention to flowers before, her eyes fixed on the far horizon, longing to be somewhere else. But for the first time in as long as she could remember, she was happy to be where she was. She had a friend in Claire and a generous benefactor in Madame Duplessis. She was coming alive with the spring, the same way the garden was.

One afternoon as they took tea in the garden, enjoying the play of sunlight through the branches and the warm breeze caressing their faces, Madame Duplessis started to sing in a soft but melodious voice:

Onn'awtewa d'ki n'on, wandaskwaentak
on-nah-wah-teh-wah do-kee non-ywah-ndah-skwa-en-tak

Ennonchien skwatrihotat n'on, wandi, onrachatha
en-non-shyen skwah-tree-hotat non-ywa-ndee-yon-rah-shah-
 thah.

"That is so beautiful!" Esther exclaimed. "What does it mean?"

"It means: 'Behold, the spirit who kept us prisoners has fled. Do not listen to it, as it corrupts our minds.'" She turned to Esther. "I sang it for you, my dear Esther. I don't know what evil has been done to you in the past, but be sure it cannot reach you here."

Esther smiled. She too was beginning to believe that she had found a home at last.

~

IT WAS ONLY WHEN Madame Lévesque came to visit that Esther was asked to tell one of her own tales of exotic places and perilous travels. As time went on she was finding this harder and harder to do, but she tried her best to please the lady who had made her present comfort and future hopes possible. This is the last tale she was able to tell her.

~

AS YOU KNOW, I spent many years at sea, first in the company of Spanish sailors and then with French ones. All this time I was forced to disguise myself, because superstition forbade the presence of women on board ship. Convinced as I was then — as I still am today — that women are capable of performing every nautical job, this exasperated me, but I continued to dress as a boy.

You may remember, Madame Lévesque, that the ship that rescued my fellow castaways and me was named *Le Lys*. At that time it was under the direction of Le Chevalier Alphonse de Pontevez, a famous French explorer, but he left the ship in Bordeaux. My new patron Monsieur Fourget and I enjoyed a few weeks of shore leave with the rest of the crew before furnishing ourselves with fresh garments and more medical supplies. Then we signed on with the same vessel again, this time to bring military supplies to the Indian port of Mahé and return home bearing the fabled silks and spices of the Orient.

I was thrilled at the prospect, as usual wanting to go to new places and see new things. We first headed back down the coast of Africa, stopping at Saint-Louis-du-Fort to take on a load of provisions and fresh water. A good many French traders from Bordeaux had settled in the town and married local women, and they all came to visit the ship, hoping to do business and receive news from home. On the third day after we arrived, a delegation of handsome Africans from the interior came looking for us. Apparently a great and learned Imam in the legendary city of Timbuktu was very ill and, all local healers having failed, a decision had been made to seek the assistance of Western medicine. Their spokesman begged our captain to help, promising him good fortune in this life and the next if he would send help back to Timbuktu with them. Reminding us that no white man had been invited to their sacred city before, the emissary recited a proverb that still thrills me strangely every time I think of it:

Salt comes from the north,
Gold comes from the south,
Money comes from the country of white people,
But the word of God
Can only be found in Timbuktu.

But our captain was unmoved. He insisted that he needed to keep his small store of medical supplies for the long and hazardous journey ahead; his first obligation was to his own crew, however much he grieved for the plight of the holy man and wished it were in his power to help him. The African pleaded most eloquently and then, when that failed, began to bargain. He brought forth a substantial amount of gold he had hidden about his person. When even his money was refused he began to call curses upon us.

I was worried about our safety but our captain insisted that we all return to our ordinary business. Unfortunately my fear proved prophetic, for later that night our ship was besieged by a heavily armed company of these same Africans, transformed from polite ambassadors to hostile soldiers. Our watch was overwhelmed, and forced to remain silent on pain of death as they led two of the invaders below to the cabin I shared with Monsieur Fourget, who was in charge of the infirmary. They roused us, compelled us to pack all our medical supplies, and hustled us off the ship, leaving behind men with flaming torches who threatened to set the vessel ablaze if anyone dared to pursue us.

It may seem strange that seafarers should be so afraid of fire, but often we had seen wooden ships burning too fast for the surrounding water to save them. So we went, unresistingly, with our captors; a few French soldiers lay portside with their throats cut and that grim sight made us glad we had decided to be docile. Under cover of darkness they made us march into the Sahel, the arid grasslands that border that town, reckoning that during the dry season, when sandstorms were prevalent, pursuit was unlikely. Although the sky blazed with millions of stars, the darkness below was complete and impenetrable. In the distance I heard a peculiar coughing noise, which I later learned was typical of camels, the beasts that were waiting for us. And off we went, from the ocean of water we knew to the ocean of sand that we knew not.

Fourget and I were mounted on a single camel, in the middle of a long column of such creatures heavily burdened with men, arms, water-skins, and bedding. Had we not been accustomed to the rocking of ships at sea we might well have found the undulating movement of these beasts unpleasant, but for us it was familiar and comforting. I was impressed by how tireless they were in the heat and dust of the desert, and reminded by them of how every place on earth is inhabited by creatures best adapted to it. For example, though camels at first appear bizarre, like hunchbacked horses badly drawn by children, they have beautiful eyes and eyelashes so long that any lady at Versailles might envy them. This feature protects the delicate organs of sight from irritation by blowing sand. For the same reason, they are able to close their nostrils with a special flap of skin, keeping their lungs free of dust. Most wonderfully of all, these creatures can store food in their humps for long treks when no food or water is to be found.

Soon enough we were to wish we had such humps ourselves. For the first few days we travelled along in almost complete silence, excited, in spite of our fear, to be going to Timbuktu. Timbuktu! The fabled land of gold and ancient wisdom no European had visited for centuries. Surely we were lucky to have been chosen for such an adventure? This at least is what we told each other, to keep our spirits up, at times when we thought we might not arrive there alive. We slept during the heat of the day and travelled mostly at night. Sometimes our captors talked quietly among themselves, sometimes they even sang, but we had little conversation except when they offered us food or directed us to mount or dismount, sleep, or rise. We had no idea where we were or where we were going, except in the direction of Timbuktu, north and east, further and further into the true desert.

Some time towards the end of the second week, when we were all sleeping in the sparse shade of an acacia tree — the plant upon which the whole wealth of that country is built, as from it they derive gum arabic — a sandstorm blew up so quickly that our captors were unable to secure us, and so violently that no one could see a thing. In the confusion of the moment, Fourget decided that we should escape. He grabbed my hand and pulled me with him the way he thought we had come. But it was impossible to have any idea at all of where we were going until the storm had abated. When it did, we were dismayed to find ourselves utterly lost, thirsty, and exhausted, and considerably worse off than we had been before. We were alone and on foot, without provisions or bedding.

After a hopeless attempt to orient ourselves in that flat

and everlasting wasteland, we decided to look for shelter and conserve our energy until night came. We crawled under a rocky ledge and tried to rest. Sand had lodged in our eyes and nostrils and ears, in every crease of our fingers, under each nail. Our mouths were so dry that there was no saliva to swallow, and we were incapable of tears though we wept in our hearts.

I reflected that Fate had spared me from death on an island inappropriately described as "desert" only to maroon me in the true Sahara. In this mood of bitter resignation I fell in and out of delirium, hardly remembering who or where I was. I have no idea how much later it was when I heard a faint jingling of bells and that familiar coughing. Assuming our captors had finally found us and grateful for the prospect of life, even life in captivity, I forced my burning eyes open only to see an unfamiliar caravan, the camels much fresher than ours, all gaily decorated with silver and scarlet ornaments, each one carrying a bundle of bright blue cloth.

At first I thought I was hallucinating. But as the camels approached, a human form was discernible astride each beast: here a graceful brown hand, there a bare foot, and many pairs of eyes, neither friendly nor hostile, merely curious, staring out from under blue turbans, blue veils, and blue robes. Convinced that any travellers so completely shrouded must surely be bandits, I prodded Monsieur Fourget, afraid to confront this new and terrible danger all by myself. He was unconscious and breathing shallowly, but eventually I roused him from his stupor. He was at first unable to sit, but after I propped him up he waved one hand in a weak gesture of greeting to the strange people gathered before us. When the first rider raised his own hand in a courteous reply, I knew that we were saved.

We soon understood that we had been rescued by the blue men of the desert, known as Tuareg or "the God forsaken" among the Arabs but "the Noble People" among themselves. Their peculiar dress is well adapted to where they live; not being camels, they must protect their faces from the sand. Indeed, they keep their mouths and noses hidden at all times, even when there is no wind. But this custom only prevails among the men, who travel for long distances on caravan routes. The women, who stay home, go barefaced, simply covering their heads after marriage.

These people are greatly feared; they are fierce swordsmen, prone to raiding others for their cattle and taking slaves in battle. They could have taken us as slaves too but we were so strange to them, with our pale skin and alien language, that it didn't occur to them. We would have been of no use to anyone in the state we were in regardless; indeed Monsieur Fourget, being so much older than I, and excessively thin even before this ordeal, did not recover. He died soon after we were rescued, unable to swallow more than a mouthful of water though he was convulsing with fever. We buried him in a shallow grave somewhere in that immensity, where only wild beasts will visit his poor bones.

Though my heart grieved bitterly, my eyes were still too dry to shed tears when I said a prayer for his departing soul. I was so sick, and so frightened of my new captors, that I cannot remember how long it took to get to their village, but eventually we reached an oasis surrounded by date palms. Outside a circle of tents, goats and chickens browsed the grass;

a few children ran up to greet us and then stopped, confused and perhaps even frightened at the sight of me. The leader of the caravan, a taciturn fellow named Az'ar, carried me into one of these dwellings where his wife promptly took charge of me. A plump woman named Faghizza, she was gaudily dressed, with silver ornaments hanging from her ears and neck. At first I was frightened of her but I soon perceived how kind and gentle she was and relaxed my vigilance.

First she stripped off my filthy garments, and then washed me as tenderly as if I had been her own daughter. This is when my tears, so long suppressed, were released. Soon her older sister, who was blind, joined us in the tent, singing the sweetest song I had ever heard in her beautiful voice. I didn't understand the words then, but I was to learn later that the song was intended to drive away evil spirits. And so with music and with love, I was welcomed into a new family.

"IS SOMETHING THE MATTER?" Madame Duplessis inquired with concern. Esther looked as though she was about to cry.

"No, nothing," Esther replied in a choked voice. "I was only thinking about the kindness of women ... like you."

"Have some more tea," suggested Madame Lévesque.

"Thank you," said Esther, gratefully. The women waited while she drained her cup and composed herself. But she was not given the chance to resume her narrative, as Claire burst into the room in great distress.

"Monsieur Varin is here to see Mademoiselle Esther on official business from the King. He says she is to come with him at once. He even has soldiers with him!"

Esther turned pale. Madame Lévesque put her arms around her, thinking she was about to faint.

"Be brave, as you always are, dear girl," she said.

Madame Duplessis kissed her on both cheeks, saying only, "May God continue to protect you."

With that, Esther left the second of her Quebec homes, never to return.

TEN

"La mejor elocuencia, la vedrá."
(*Truth is the greatest eloquence.*)

FOR THEIR JOURNEY TO the Intendant's palace they were accompanied by a military escort, one soldier sitting up with the driver and another clinging on behind. Esther was unnerved by their presence, especially as Varin said nothing to her about the purpose of the trip, only staring out the window of the *calèche* and pulling his legs back to avoid brushing against her skirt. When they arrived he did not hand her down politely as he would any other woman but left her to struggle awkwardly by herself, then gestured that she must follow him around the back of the building, to the prison wing.

Esther had never been there before, having avoided the place entirely during her autumn's residence with Hocquart.

The Intendant himself had reminded her occasionally that she ought to have been stuck in there rather than running around at liberty in his house, but she had never taken these comments very seriously; the man's innate kindness was too obvious. And living with Madame Duplessis had only made her feel more secure. How foolish she had been to take her safety for granted! Clearly Varin had learned who she was and intended to punish her severely for it.

No sooner had the door closed behind them than he motioned for Esther to stand in front of the big desk where Monsieur Hocquart sat, an inscrutable expression upon his face. It had been more than four months since she had last seen him but she could not think of him as her enemy.

Varin made a great show of opening a letter from France, then cleared his throat and said, "Well, girl, it's time to go home. Your family is quite worried about you."

"What family, Monsieur Varin?" asked Esther. Her heart was pounding so loudly she was sure he must be able to hear it. Could this be the same man who had flirted with her, flattered her, and sought to seduce her when she arrived on these shores? She could see nothing in his face now but undisguised revulsion.

"The family of David Brandeau, a Jewish merchant of Bayonne," he spat, as though the very word "Jewish" left a foul taste in his mouth.

Hocquart too was repelled, but also fascinated.

The only Jews he had ever had dealings with were members of the Gradis family, great merchants whose services were essential to the colonial shipping industry. They lived in the Bordeaux region which, having been under English occupation at the time France expelled its Jews, was the only part of the country where those of their nation were permitted to reside. They themselves were very powerful; Abraham Gradis had even been received at court, for the King relied on his knowledge and wealth to extend the French Empire. Gradis was a cultured man, though of course ambitious and greedy as all his race was.

Hocquart had heard terrible things about Jews all his life, things too terrible to imagine, involving human sacrifice and satanic rituals. Although these were only folk superstitions, their taint attached to anyone suspected of being Jewish, including converts and the children of converts. Furthermore, the Code Noir explicitly prohibited Jewish emigration to New France. Hocquart had asked Esther if she were a Huguenot but it had not occurred to him even once that she might be a Jew. He felt foolish, realizing how many signs he had overlooked: her food aversions; her obsession with reading; her disinclination to attend Mass and, when dragged there on occasion by Marie-Thérèse, her refusal to make her confession; her odd accent; the sense he had that she was hiding a terrible secret. The stress etched prematurely on her face from maintaining a constant vigilance.

He gazed at that familiar olive-skinned face appraisingly. There were no signs of corruption in her dark eyes, nothing more than fear. By contrast, the upward curl of those full lips hinted at a refusal to take anything seriously, even her current predicament. The girl might be odd and unfeminine, she might be a manipulative liar, but he knew in his heart that she was not evil; on the contrary, Esther was, in some peculiar way, his friend.

Hocquart felt an unaccustomed surge of tenderness. His life had been fuller, if more complicated, when Esther Brandeau had lived in his house. Inspired by her tales of distant lands, he had toyed with the idea of applying for another posting himself: the Indies, East and West; Africa; the Pacific Islands. He was still young enough to travel; why should he stay here his whole life, bickering with Beauharnois? Esther had reminded him how vast the globe was and how little of it he had seen so far. And even after he'd forbidden himself the enchantment of her storytelling, he had continued to relish her presence in his library, seeing her lost in thought or reading a book, her legs childishly drawn up under her skirt, her face rapt with pleasure. Sometimes he would pick up a volume she had abandoned when he came in later in the evening, searching the pages for whatever it was that had absorbed her. And it was her voice, soft and thrilling, that he heard in his head as he read the strange words inside. It was her voice that made the world seem so welcoming, so full of possibilities.

Whatever she had run away from must have been truly terrible; knowing that she was Jewish only made him more certain of that. He still had an instinct to protect her, despite everything. He decided that he would insist that she stay here until they were able to determine the truth about this David Brandeau. Surely there must be more than one family with the name "Brandeau" in all of France. It didn't sound like a Jewish name. Was it? There were perfectly valid reasons for a responsible official to question this new report, and he intended to invoke each one of them.

But it was impossible. Varin loved to gossip. If he had not

spread the word already, which was unlikely, he would tell the world soon enough that Esther Brandeau, the girl who had come to New France dressed as a boy, was also a filthy Jew. Hocquart's reputation would be in jeopardy throughout the colony, which would mean a victory for Beauharnois. He glanced at the younger man's shining chestnut mane, worn long and tied in back with a black velvet ribbon, and wondered briefly what he did to keep it so healthy. His own hair was already sparse and grey under his itchy white wig. He had never been handsome, never rich. And now that he was old, all he had was his position. Hocquart began to speak, hoping the right words would come to him in time.

"How reliable is this report?"

"It is signed and witnessed."

"And what of the man himself? Does he have a good reputation?"

"I know nothing of him, I admit, Monsieur Hocquart. But why would anyone lie about losing a daughter?"

"I can think of many reasons. He could have done away with his real daughter and be covering up a murder. He might want an unpaid servant in his home."

"Clearly you have developed an imagination to rival the girl's," Varin sneered.

"I am only eager to see justice done, Monsieur Varin. You would do well to remember that. There are some unsavoury rumours making their way around town about your own shady dealings."

Varin was taken aback. He had always considered Hocquart a dull administrator, someone to tolerate but never to fear.

True, he had come over with the man on the ill-fated *Eléphant*, and had been repeatedly promoted under his patronage; yet whenever sides had needed to be taken he'd sided with the Marquis de La Boische, who seemed more impressive as an ally and more formidable as an enemy. It had never occurred to him that his flattery of the Governor General might alienate the Intendant, nor that the latter could have any real capacity to do him harm.

"I am only concerned for the reputation of your government, Monsieur Hocquart."

"As are we all, Monsieur Varin," Hocquart replied. "So we will take a little longer to investigate these new claims. There will still be plenty of time to send Esther back to Bayonne, if that is indeed where she comes from, before the port freezes over again."

"But what do you propose to do with her in the meantime?"

Hocquart had no answer to this. Despite his duties as a magistrate and the number of criminals he had condemned to jail for offences less grave than Esther Brandeau's, he had never felt as responsible for another human being's fate as he did for hers. And then the solution came to him. It was so obvious that he felt foolish for not having seen it before.

"She shall go to the Ursuline nuns," he replied, with relief and conviction. "After all, it is their mission to bring converts into the church."

Esther had stood silently with her head bowed during this exchange, having nothing to say in her own defence: Jews were not allowed in New France, and she no longer had the heart to deny that she was one. For whatever reason, Monsieur

Hocquart was prepared to give her another chance to stay. She would take it.

But she was filled with terror at the ordeal that awaited her. All her life she had been threatened with the Inquisition, and here it was at last. There really was no way to avoid Fate; fleeing was another way of running towards it. Wasn't that what Sophocles had written about King Oedipus? She remembered listening to a heated discussion between her older brothers about the conflict between the will of man and that of the gods in the philosophy of the ancient Greeks. Well, no philosophy would save her now. And no fantastic story she could dream up would change official policy. She could only remain silent, and hope for the best.

∾

WHEN ESTHER HAD FIRST seen Marie-Charlotte de Ramezay *dite* de Saint-Claude de la Croix skating with nonchalant skill on the frozen river, she had been thrilled. It seemed wonderful that, in this country, a woman could rise to a position of such authority and respect. Her reading of the life of Marie de l'Incarnation had only confirmed her gratitude that she had picked New France as the place to start her new life; if other women could be strong and independent here, surely she could too. She had begun to overcome her childhood dread of nuns and started to see them as potential role models: intellectual Amazons travelling places other women were forbidden to go, doing things other women were prevented from doing.

But as she spooned up watery pea soup in the convent

dining hall, any fantasy about life among a fearless tribe of scholar-warriors quickly evaporated. Worse than the scanty meals themselves was the fact that they were held in complete silence, broken only by the reading of a chapter of sacred text by an elderly nun who compensated for her deafness by shouting in a hoarse monotone. Listening to her was an ordeal, but no one was permitted to leave the room until the reading was complete, including those nuns who had duties to perform.

Esther herself had no occupation. For four long days she waited for someone to tell her where to go and what to do. She was unsure whether she was even permitted to wander about the building, although she peeked into as many rooms as she could. The convent was vast, a three-storey structure of solid stone with balconies encircling it and many outbuildings, a miniature village of women. As far as she could tell, the top floor consisted entirely of cells like hers; even the long-term residents were given no greater material comfort than new arrivals. Above the top floor was a low attic full of drying laundry. The middle floor, by contrast, comprised large rooms bustling with activity. In one of these rooms, a group of nuns were busy embroidering surplices and other decorative cloths for the church with exquisite flowers and gold and silver thread; in another, a class of novices took religious instruction; in yet another, a few very old women were cared for tenderly by their younger and healthier sisters. The lower level held bakeries and kitchens and storehouses of all kinds, and in it another community, this one made up of female servants, was hard at work.

Esther was happiest in the dining hall, not because the food was good — it wasn't — but because it was properly heated, unlike her room. Though she kept her door open, hoping to receive some warmth from the woodstove burning in the corridor, the cell to which she had been assigned remained frigid. So she spent most of her time in bed, curled up under the covers for warmth. Besides the bed itself, which was fitted with good quality linens and a thick blanket, her other furniture consisted of a plain pine desk and two hard chairs. The room's only ornament was a wooden crucifix nailed to the wall and the only entertainment it offered was a small volume of the *Lives of the Saints*, illustrated with woodcuts depicting many ingenious varieties of martyrdom in stark black and white detail. Since she had first learned to read, Esther had taken refuge in literature; denied other books, she resorted to this one.

She first looked up Saint Ursula, wanting to know something about Madame Duplessis's favourite martyr, the one to whom the convent was dedicated. Esther found to her surprise that, like her, Ursula had preferred literature and travel to more typically feminine pursuits. Despite these similarities, however, Ursula's example was not encouraging. She had been tortured to death for rejecting marriage and refusing to denounce her faith.

Esther flipped through the book looking for someone whose fate was less dire but found only page after page of horror. Surely the nuns were taunting her? For here was the stuff of her childhood nightmares: the rat-infested dungeons, the burnings with hot coals, the tearing of flesh with pincers, the *strappado*, the rack, the bonfires of writhing bodies. Image after image depicted the same scenarios that had driven her own people from Spain and Portugal and scattered them across the globe. Clearly the Inquisition had turned to the ancient Romans for guidance on how to torture people. What had been inflicted on Christians then they now, in their turn, inflicted upon Jews.

And she had delivered herself right into their hands.

She would have been better off had she stayed at home. She might have been wretched, but at least she would have been safe. The Jews of Bayonne had *Lettres Patents* from King Louis himself; they were allowed to live in peace, despised but tolerated, taxed unfairly but unbroken in body or spirit. It was a lively enough place with a varied community of shopkeepers and tradesmen and chocolatiers; the weather was pleasant and the food was consistently good, with more variety of fruits and vegetables than was attainable in Quebec with its short growing season. Remembering her relative comfort back in France, Esther gave in to despair. Her sleep was disrupted by lurid dreams and the daylight hours suffused with long-suppressed loneliness.

If only she had one other book, whether a serious account of a voyage, a romance full of magic and adventure, or even a volume of love poems, she could have lost herself in someone else's story and shut out the terrible voices that filled her head. Voices reminding her of all the things she was not permitted to do; voices insisting that she was worthless and unwanted; a chorus of voices sneering that it didn't matter that nobody knew where she was since not one person in the world cared what happened to her. She thought she was about to go mad when a tiny novice no more than sixteen years old, her fair complexion spoiled by acne, arrived to take her to Mother Claude's office. The girl, trembling with nervousness at such unaccustomed responsibility, whispered to Esther to be polite and only speak when she was spoken to.

"But you have spoken to me, haven't you?" Esther replied.

The novice was so startled at being addressed that she blushed redder than her pimples and scurried away, leaving Esther to wait alone outside the great lady's door for another thirty minutes. She presumed this delay was intended to arouse her fear; if so, it had succeeded. Esther paced back and forth, back and forth, trying her best to pray, wishing she believed that prayer would work. But even in this convent, surrounded by the genuinely devout, she doubted that any deity powerful enough to have created the world was interested in the fate of individual creatures. God hadn't saved those early Christian martyrs, nor those of her own people whose fate had been modelled on theirs. Why, then, would he be inspired to rescue someone as insignificant as Esther Brandeau?

All she could see ahead of her was a life of imprisonment or a painful death. Saint Ursula had been shot with an arrow while her eleven thousand virgin companions were beheaded; Saint Lawrence, after whom the great river of this land was named, had been broiled alive on a griddle. Esther was still debating which of the options awaiting her would be preferable when the door opened with a portentous wailing of hinges, and she was summoned into the mother superior's presence.

"You are to address me as Mother Claude," the nun said, the extreme plainness of her face given unfortunate emphasis by the starched white guimpe and bandeau circling it. But under the broad forehead her hazel eyes sparkled with intelligence, and there was no sign of hatred in them. Esther felt relief flood through her. Perhaps martyrdom was not to be her destiny after all. Still, she was determined to hold herself aloof in case the woman's pleasant smile hid sharp jaws waiting to snap down on her.

"It seems odd that nuns call themselves 'mothers' when they have vowed not to have any children."

"I have heard reports of your insolence," the nun replied sharply.

"I didn't mean to be insolent, Mother Claude. Usually when people think I am being rude, I am only making a factual observation."

"Do not assume you that you understand the meaning of what you see, Esther."

"Indeed, I understand very little of what I see in this world," Esther replied wearily.

Mother Claude, thinking the girl looked frightened despite her mask of bravado, decided not to confront her further until she had settled into her new routine. She had many years of experience taming recalcitrant savages; how much more difficult could a French girl be, even a Jewish one? It was true that she had never met a Jew before this, but despite her unfortunate lineage this child was undoubtedly more rational than a Native, and therefore more amenable to true doctrine. Besides, Madame Duplessis had spoken of her fondly and she was no fool.

She sent Esther on her way with a couple of texts to study, and told her that they would meet in one week's time to discuss what she must do to prove herself worthy of being accepted into the Church.

~

DEPRIVED OF THE SOLACE of literature, conversation, and affection, all of which she had grown accustomed to at Madame Duplessis's house, Esther sank into melancholy. There was little of interest or variety in convent life. The nuns rose early to pray, ate simply, and then went about their business of civilizing the Natives and proselytizing to the old and sick, leaving her alone to study in her cell when not called to Mass. Despite spending many hours in collective worship, she felt more isolated in a houseful of girls her own age — most of whom were afraid of her, scornful of her, or both — than she had been on the *Saint Michel* with a crew of rough, adventurous men.

For these reasons, she looked forward to her weekly study sessions with Mother Claude; at least when she was with the mother superior she could participate in an actual dialogue. It was a great relief to be talked to as an intelligent person and not simply condemned as a sinner; to be allowed to ask questions rather than being told to repent. The tough old nun was quite different from anyone else Esther had met in Quebec. She was not threatened by anything Esther repre-sented because she herself had rejected the customary female roles of subordination and maternity. In her own way, she had achieved as much responsibility as Hocquart and as much influence as Beauharnois, without having to suffer the humi-liations of the one or the physical dangers of the other. And not even Varin was so foolish as to try to seduce her or put her in her place.

Varin was wiser in that regard than Esther, who challenged the nun's religious convictions with stories of distant lands and alternative deities. However, for someone so steeped in myth and symbol, Mother Claude was strangely impervious to the charms of narrative. And despite her intellectual keenness, she was not very curious about the world beyond New France. She claimed to have more than enough to keep her occupied at home, and felt that daydreaming about life elsewhere was a waste of time; almost a sin.

Mother Claude challenged equally Esther's recalcitrance. She had her memorize the Apostle's Creed, the Lord's Prayer, and the Hail Mary, so that Esther could meditate upon the Joyful Mysteries, the Sorrowful Mysteries, and the Glorious Mysteries while telling her rosary. Already familiar with of these prayers from her residence with Madame Duplessis, Esther recited them by rote with no expression in her voice, as though reciting a list of items to pick up at the market rather than the central tenets of a religion.

> *I believe in God, the Father Almighty,*
> *the Creator of heaven and earth,*
> *and in Jesus Christ, His only Son, our Lord:*
> *Who was conceived by the Holy Spirit,*
> *born of the Virgin Mary,*
> *suffered under Pontius Pilate,*
> *was crucified, died, and was buried.*
> *He descended into hell.*

The third day He arose again from the dead.
He ascended into heaven
and sits at the right hand of God the Father Almighty,
whence He shall come to judge the living and the dead.
I believe in the Holy Spirit, the holy Catholic Church,
the communion of saints,
the forgiveness of sins,
the resurrection of the body,
and life everlasting.
Amen.

Her tone irritated the nun, who was unwavering in her insistence that conversion was Esther's best — indeed her only — option.

"You obviously have no commitment to your own faith, since you ran away from it," she snapped in frustration one day, "so why are you so resistant to the One True Church?"

"I didn't run away from my faith, Mother Claude," Esther objected. "I ran away from the limitations that faith subjected me to."

"Can you explain the distinction?"

"If you let me tell you a story."

"As I have told you before, I am not interested in hearing any of your stories unless they are true."

"This one is."

"Very well, then."

So Esther began. For once she did not close her eyes, but met the nun's candid gaze steadily.

∾

I GREW UP IN Saint Esprit, a suburb of Bayonne, amidst the community of Portuguese Jews. You may not know that area, Mother Claude; it's in the Bordeaux region where the best wine comes from. We were tolerated because of our usefulness to His Majesty; given our origins as refugees from the Inquisition, we were able to facilitate maritime trade down the coast because we spoke the Iberian languages. My father was the manager of a warehouse holding the wealth of the Atlantic trade, a busy and a prosperous man and therefore able to pay the heavy taxes the King was pleased to inflict upon him, as upon all Jews.

As is typical of that community, I received a good education, learning to read and write at a young age despite the prospect of doing nothing more with my knowledge than raising a family. Indeed, there is a proverb among our people: "La ija del Djudio, no keda sin kazar," which means, "No daughter of a Jew remains unmarried." We have no tradition of nuns as you do, Mother Claude, being bound instead by the command-ment to go forth and multiply.

In accordance with this commandment, my father and mother decided to send me to Amsterdam, where my mother's sister had arranged a marriage for me with a much older man, a widower, most of whose children were older than me. I went weeping and wailing, but went nonetheless, being a girl and therefore having no control whatsoever over my own life.

The boat I sailed on was Dutch, captained by a man named Geoffrey. Almost as soon as we sailed out of port a storm blew up, and we ran aground on the sandbanks of Bayonne. I don't know what happened to the others on board that ship, but I was saved from drowning and brought to shore by one of the seamen, who lodged me with a widow named Catherine Churriau in Biarritz. I stayed with her for fifteen days, recovering from my injuries. When I confided to this kind woman that I dared not return home because I was to be married against my will, she lent me some of her son's clothes. In this capacity and under the name of Pierre Mausiette — "Pierre" because it was a rock-solid Christian name, if you will forgive the pun, and "Mausiette" because I was taken out of the water like a female Moses — I went to Bordeaux, where I engaged as a cabin boy on a ship destined for Nantes.

For a long time I travelled up and down the west coast of France, sometimes finding employment as a sailor, sometimes as a tailor or a baker. Although most of my jobs were tedious and my life was lonely, I was free. I no longer had to stay hidden indoors as other girls did, away from hostile eyes, subservient to men. Nor was I restricted to certain trades and certain places merely by virtue of being a Jew. You cannot imagine how big the world suddenly seemed to me, how unlimited the possibilities! All my life I'd longed to live free from the prejudice of others and to travel. Now, because of a lucky accident or the hand of God — you may decide which as you like, Mother Claude — both of my heart's desires had been fulfilled at once.

And then I was arrested, being mistaken for another lad with the same name. Although I was released as soon as my accuser saw my face and realized that I was the wrong person, my masquerade had come very close to being exposed. For this reason I changed my name again, this time to Jacques Lafargue — "Jacques" because it was a joke, and "La Fargue" because I was a female smith, reforging my identity — and determined to travel to New France, where I thought there would be less chance of discovery and more scope for meaningful employment.

~

ESTHER LOOKED UP AT Mother Claude expectantly.

"So here I am."

"Far from supporting your claim that you were not running away from your faith, Esther, this tale makes it clear that you have never been a very good Jew."

"You are right," Esther replied sadly. "I have never been very good."

"Oh my dear child, it sounds like you are finally ready for the sacrament of confession. You will find it a great relief to unburden your soul." Mother Claude's homely face was vivid with joy.

"I am sorry, Mother Claude. I didn't intend to mislead you," said Esther.

"What do you mean?"

"I was only conceding that I have done some bad things. For example, eating pork. When I was sick, Madame Churriau gave me bacon without my knowing it; I thought it was delicious until I knew what it was. I tried to spit it up, but it was too late."

"Why do I keep wasting my time with you, Esther?" Mother Claude asked, slamming her prayer book shut in a rare display of vexation. "You would be wise to consider the situation realistically."

"I beg your pardon?"

"You keep saying you do not want to go home. Well, why would you, if your only prospect is rejoining a nation that bears the curse of having murdered Our Lord?"

Esther protested, "But Mother Claude, the Bible says it was the Romans who killed Jesus, the same way they killed the other martyrs, like Saint Lawrence, later."

The nun was dumbfounded. In all her years of saving souls no one had ever argued scripture against her, not even the most cunning of the Indians entrusted to her care. Clearly something more drastic was needed to bring out this girl's fears and vulnerabilities — something that would reduce her to such helplessness that she would gladly take refuge in the Church.

"You say you wish for meaningful employment, Esther? Very well. From now on, you will assist in the lunatic ward of the hospital. I imagine you will feel quite at home there."

Esther stared at the floor. She had drawn out the verbal battle with Mother Claude as long as she could, but had clearly overestimated the woman's patience. But she couldn't help it; she was able neither to avow a faith she didn't hold nor reject her own tradition on the basis of ignorant lies. Too many of her people had been murdered, or subjected to unspeakable torture, by Mother Claude's beloved Church. The year before Esther set sail for New France, twelve Marranos had been burned at the stake in Lisbon, the city the Brandãos had originally come from. The city where some of their relatives probably still lived in hiding, fearful every day of fueling a similar *auto de fé* themselves. If she were to convert to Christianity it would make a mockery of the sufferings of all those other Jews.

She could have explained this conviction to Mother Claude if she tried, but she doubted it was worth the effort. The woman had not become Mother Superior by conceding the rights of others to practise different faiths. But there was something else Esther Brandeau knew she would never be able to make Mother Claude understand, as much as she admired the woman and wished for her approval: if she converted, it would make her own life meaningless. It would mean that instead of gaining freedom she had lost it. And freedom was the only thing she had; freedom was her true religion, and she was not prepared to give it up. So she remained silent, and resolved to take whatever punishment awaited her.

ELEVEN

"Cuando ganéden está accerado,
guehinam está siempre abierto."
(*The Garden of Eden may be closed,*
but Hell is always open.)

ONCE UPON A TIME, there was a scholarly Jew who was well versed in every art but magic. Hearing that all the greatest magicians in the world lived in Egypt, he decided to travel there to study with them. On the first night of his journey he arrived at a small roadside inn. The innkeeper showed him to a comfortable room with a soft featherbed and asked him how long he would be staying. The traveller said that he would have to leave early in the morning as he was going all the way to Egypt to study magic.

The innkeeper immediately announced that he himself was a famous magician and could teach the scholar everything he wanted to know. But the scholar thought that the innkeeper, who was old and bent and bald as an egg, could not be as powerful as he claimed. The scholar mocked him, suggesting that he use his magic to make the bill disappear.

It is never a good idea to make fun of a magician, as the scholar learned soon after. The innkeeper left him to unpack his few belongings and returned with a large bowl of water, inviting him to clean up before dinner was served. As soon as the scholar bent over the bowl to wash his face, he lost his balance and fell in. The bowl had been transformed into a vast ocean and he found himself swimming frantically for shore, though there was no land anywhere in sight. The next thing he knew a terrible storm blew up, with clamorous thunder, lightning brighter than the sun, and waves hundreds of feet high. As they swept over the scholar he was convinced that he was about to drown, so he recited his final prayers.

How long he floated, salt tears mingling with salt water, he did not know. But eventually he heard something. He flipped over onto his belly and saw faintly, in the distance, a dark shape moving towards him. It was a ship! The sailors on deck heard his cries, threw him a rope, and hauled him aboard. They gave him dry clothes and a big glass of rum to drink, and, after they had talked with him for a time, confessed amazement at his vast knowledge and his fluency in many languages. They invited him to come home with them to their native land, where scholars were revered above all other men.

So he went to their homeland, where he was received with great respect. He became the governor over that distant country and ruled wisely for many years. He married and had six children, three boys and three girls, and forgot all about his intention to go to Egypt to study magic.

One day, the scholar's adopted country was conquered by the army of an evil sultan and he was captured and taken into slavery. This sultan was very cruel; it amused him to watch his foreign prisoners working day after day in the blazing sun, building a huge wall around his kingdom to keep themselves in and everybody else out. When a slave died — as they often did, for the work was hard and they were fed nothing but dry bread and water — his bones were mixed into the clay to make the bricks stronger. An armed guard stood watch over the slaves while they worked during the day and while they slept at night. No one had ever escaped captivity, so the poor scholar despaired of ever seeing his beloved wife and children again.

After years of this misery, and long after he had given up all hope of rescue, fortune suddenly favoured him. He was left unsupervised for a few minutes and ran off into the desert. The soldiers of the king chose not to pursue him, certain that he would soon become lost in that endless wasteland and die of hunger and thirst. And indeed, after wandering for hours with no idea at all of where he was going, the scholar grew weary and took shelter in a cave, where he fell into a deep sleep.

He had no idea how long he had been sleeping when a strange sound awakened him. A marvellous golden bird stood in the entrance of the cave, singing, "Come away, come away." Convinced that the creature was talking to him, the scholar followed it out of the cave. The bird stayed out of his reach, fluttering from rock to rock, eventually arriving at a lush oasis surrounded by tall date palms heavy with ripe fruit. Kneeling down to drink, the scholar saw, in the unmoving water, the reflection of someone behind him. It was the bald old innkeeper with whom he had spent a night many years ago on his way to Egypt.

"Monsieur," said the innkeeper, "You've been washing your face in this bowl for a very long time. Your dinner is growing cold. Won't you come downstairs to eat now?"

And so, realizing his error, the scholar decided to stay with the innkeeper and learn the art of magic from him.

∼

WHEN ESTHER BROKE OFF her story with satisfaction, proud of having provided some entertainment to the lunatic ward, she was disconcerted at the near riot that broke out around her. Instead of being soothed by her tale-telling as she had assumed they would be, the inmates were more agitated than ever.

"Come away, come away," shrieked one as she swooped around the room, flapping her arms like a demented bird. A toothless woman with a face like an old boot and a mane of luxurious red hair, she had suffocated her eighteenth child at birth. Her other children missed her dreadfully but the hospital would not allow her to go home, and she had grown more and more frantic as the weeks went by.

"Come away, come away," several other patients chimed in, imitating her. The more timid ones started to cry at the commotion around them, and one old man howled on all fours like a dog.

"You wicked girl," shouted Sister Agnes, who was trying, unsuccessfully, to catch the flapping woman. "It will take all afternoon to settle them down again."

It was lucky that Doctor Lévesque was in residence that day. Being one of the few local doctors to have been trained in France, he ordinarily worked at the Hôtel-Dieu where respectable people were sent when they fell ill. However, he insisted on visiting the Hôpital Général once a week to supervise the ministrations of the nursing sisters to the dregs of society: the poor, the disabled, the criminal, the insane. As she got to know the man better, Esther had become more and more impressed by both his expertise and his compassion.

Doctor Lévesque scolded Esther, gently, for telling the inmates stories, reminding her how much trouble they had distinguishing reality and fantasy. He tied the howling man to a chair with soft restraints, wiped the spittle from his face tenderly, and continued his rounds of the ward. He comforted a sobbing girl, examined the throat of a rigid man who claimed to be unable to swallow food, gave a sugar pill here and a pat on the back there until all the patients were satisfied that something, however inadequate, had been done for them. As soon as he moved on to the next inmate, the ones he left behind dissolved into tears or started ranting incoherently; however, for the brief moment they had his attention they became calmer and more articulate, and it became possible to see the suffering individual under the mask of madness.

"How do you manage to keep your temper?" Esther inquired, after one patient, a stunted deaf-mute of indeterminate age and gender, tried to bite him.

"Gratitude."

"For what?"

"For not being them."

In all her months of discussing the virtues of submission with Madame Duplessis or the possibility of redemption after death with Mother Claude, Esther had not felt as moved as she did upon hearing this. As much as she respected both women, she was not drawn to the kind of mysticism demanded by their version of religion. Esther wanted to see the effects of her actions in this world, not the next. She had no interest in the afterworld and believed neither in angels nor demons; she only wanted for her life to mean something. The doctor's practical philanthropy appealed to her in a way that sermons about sin and redemption did not.

"You are a very good man," she said.

"No," he replied. "Just a very good doctor."

"I would like to learn from you to be of use. If I make myself indispensable, Monsieur Hocquart may not send me away."

"I doubt it. The law states that only Catholics may live in New France." The bitterness in his tone was unmistakable, and it took Esther by surprise.

"Do you think the law is unfair, Doctor?" she blurted out.

"It doesn't matter what I think, does it?"

Inadvertently Esther found herself looking around to make sure none of the nursing sisters were in the vicinity and had overheard them. Luckily they were alone; perhaps that was why the doctor had felt free to say such a thing to her. Or maybe it was because she was a Jew, an outsider, and therefore could not get him into trouble for his free thinking.

Regardless of the reason, she was grateful. It had been rare, in her experience, to meet anyone else who saw life the way she did. She determined at once to become the best possible assistant to Doctor Lévesque, and worked twice as hard as she had before: carrying his medical supplies from room to room, consoling patients in his absence, feeding the catatonic, bathing the incontinent. It was ironic that having fled a life of domestic labour back home she should be consigned to one on the other side of the ocean, but she hoped that at least in this place her work might be valued.

It was not all tedious. She was allowed to play marbles with the younger patients and chess with the older ones, and she heard a number of wild tales — some wilder than those she herself was accustomed to telling, but which she no longer dared indulge in. This was her favourite part of the job: she was rapt with wonder as a young boy recounted with absolute conviction and considerable descriptive power how he flew around the silent countryside at night when others slept, grazing the treetops; as a wizened man with a matted beard explained that he was the illegitimate son of the King, exiled because his mother had fallen out of favour at court. There seemed to be an extraordinary number of aristocrats in hiding among the lunatics, and an equal quantity of prophets and holy men. And they all liked Esther, because she alone among the nursing staff not only listened patiently to their complicated histories but also solicited further details.

When she wasn't being entertained by the patients' delusions and flattered by their proposals of marriage, or sponging their feverish limbs and holding the basin for them to be bled, Esther continued to enjoy her occasional conversations with the doctor. He had a vein of dark humour that echoed her view of the world, and he did not seem at all bothered by the fact that she was Jewish — unlike the nursing sisters, who made insulting comments all the time.

Esther was surprised to realize, in retrospect, the lack of hostility Mother Claude had displayed towards her. Perhaps it was because she was so secure in her own faith; certainly she was less credulous than these other nuns, who were prepared to believe the most bizarre things about her. "Show us your horns, Queen Esther," they would say, or "Would you like us to save the patients' blood for you to use in your Passover rituals?" Whenever Doctor Lévesque was around he would reprimand them, but they still managed to hiss venom at Esther when he was out of hearing. She thought of complaining to Mother Claude at their weekly tutorials, but did not want to draw too much attention to her situation. No one was talking about sending her back to France anymore, and she intended to keep it that way. This was her first summer in Quebec but she hoped it would not be her last.

It was amazing how hot the weather had become after the long winter and tremulous spring, and it was only getting hotter with each day. Esther began sweating freely even when she did not exert herself. She tried to do her chores with the same commitment as before but her energy flagged and she became more and more exhausted. She felt as though she were stumbling through fog, and her whole body hurt. When Sister Agnes yelled at her for being lazy and incompetent, a typical parasitical Jew, she asked if she might go lie down for a while, then found herself unable to get out of bed all that day and the next. On the third morning, Doctor Lévesque himself came to examine her.

"What is the matter, Esther?" he asked.

"I am so tired that I can hardly move. I can't stop shivering even though I'm burning up with fever, and my right arm hurts."

He rolled up her sleeve to find red streaks climbing up her arm from a deep cut at the base of her thumb. The limb was hot and swollen.

"How did you do this?"

"One of the patients broke a chamber pot and I cut myself picking up the pieces."

"You appear to have blood poisoning," he said. Although he spoke calmly, she could tell he was worried.

"Will I die?" she asked, with no more emotion than if she had asked him the time of day. Doctor Lévesque was alarmed. Such lassitude suggested that the infection had already progressed quite far, so far that her reason was affected; surely it wasn't possible that any girl so young had no desire to live?

"Not if I can help it," he said. "But you will probably get worse before you get better."

Esther collapsed against the pillow, although one part of her still insisted that she pay attention so that she would learn what to do in this kind of medical emergency. Doctor Lévesque was already tying a tourniquet about her wrist and calling out curt instructions to the nursing sisters to bring boiling water and clean rags and medicinal salves. Then he lanced the wound to release a stream of pus and blood, squeezing it so hard that Esther cried out in pain as the others crowded around him. They were all black and white, so black and white it made her dizzy. Their faces frightened her, ghostly, floating above their cloaked bodies; why hadn't she noticed how *strange* the nuns looked before? She tried to explain this revelation to the doctor, but he told her to keep quiet and save her strength.

What was that smell? Something sweet and familiar, something from faraway France. Lavender! Someone was rubbing her sore arm with a healing lotion and binding it tightly; the aroma was so pervasive that she feared she might vomit. She closed her eyes, submitting to a wave of exhaustion that carried her away like the ocean, drowning her and then letting her rise to the surface again and again until she no longer knew if it were day or night, winter or summer, until she no longer knew who she was, or where.

She dreamed of being tossed by a violent storm that swept away everyone she'd known or loved, a storm that left her sodden clothes sticking to her limbs and her mind full of terror. Maybe she was on Noah's ark; there were chattering apes there, peeling bananas with their feet, and solemn camels batting their long eyelashes, and a fierce golden lion whose red mouth opened into an enormous cave which swallowed her alive. It was so dark inside the cave that she could see nothing, but there were voices echoing all around her, calling many names: *Estrella, Esther, Aissata, Estella, Esteban, Edza, Aziza* ...

At one point she was lifted up and carried outside; she could smell flowers and trees and feel the warm summer air on her skin, so light and gentle after her clammy bedding. She struggled back to consciousness, whimpering, trying to open her eyes.

"Don't worry, little Esther," she heard a man's voice say. "You are coming home with me."

She tried to speak, to thank him, but nothing emerged

but "*Gracias.*" Surely that was the wrong word? But the man seemed to understand what she meant, for he replied, "*De nada.*" When the warm breeze ruffled her hair, she heard herself cry out in the same half-forgotten tongue as though she were someone else. When she was settled comfortably into the back of a carriage with blankets heaped around her, she found herself drowsily crooning a lullaby from another life:

Y anoche, mi madre
cuando me eché a acordar
soñabo un sueño ...

And when she stopped, forgetting what came next, the man finished the verse for her:

tan dulce era de contar:
que me adormía
y a orias del mar.

So rocking in the back of the carriage as though she were back on board ship, she drifted off to sleep.

∽

SHE WAS ROCKING, STILL rocking. And someone was singing to her in that deep language her body knew so well. The song made her feel small and protected; the song enfolded her in her mother's familiar arms. Esther had missed her mother terribly but here she was, after all this time, summoned by the words of the song. *Mama!*

There, there, a voice said to her, *go to sleep, little one. Sleep, and soon you will be well.* Then a gentle hand brushed her damp hair back from her burning forehead, the way her mother used to when she was small, when she was sick, before she got better but her mother didn't. The hand touched her as she hadn't been touched in years. So she slept, deeply and gratefully. She slept as though nothing bad could happen to her ever again. Sometimes she felt herself being sponged with cool water, and she drank gratefully of any liquid that was held up to her parched lips. When she settled back to sleep and the bad dreams went away, all she remembered was her mother's face: a face she thought she had forgotten long ago.

TWELVE

"Si neviim no somos, de neviim venimos."
(We may not be prophets, but we are descended from them.)

LIKE CLOUDS SHIFTING IN a high wind, the startlingly vivid dreams dispersed, leaving behind only the welcome memory of her mother's face. Esther woke up to find herself in an unfamiliar bed in unfamiliar clothes. She sat up — light-headed, confused, but herself again — and drank greedily from a full glass of water sitting on a table within arm's reach.

On the same table there was also a delicate blue and white porcelain plate holding two biscuits. She slowly ate one, then the other, savouring their sweetness and the way they dissolved so lightly upon her tongue. She had no idea how long it had been since she had last eaten but she was very hungry. She finished the glass of water and then, as more time passed, began to grow restless. Assuming she must be back at Madame Duplessis's house despite the fact that she did not recognize anything around her, she called out tentatively, "Claire?"

Instead it was Madame Lévesque who came bustling in.

"I am delighted to see you looking so well, Esther," she said, her rosy face aglow over a dress of brilliant red satin.

"Are you the one who has been taking care of me?" Esther asked, abashed.

"Yes, my dear."

"Why?"

"Gabriel and I thought you would recover better here than in the hospital."

"Really?"

"Really," Madame Lévesque laughed. "Why do you find it so hard to accept that people care about you?"

Esther swallowed. "It's too hard to explain."

"Try. It is not good for you to hold things in; it will only make you sicker. And believe me, I am very good at keeping secrets." Madame Lévesque sat on edge of the bed and took the girl's cold hands in hers.

"Tell me about your real family, Esther."

Esther looked down at their hands, entwined together. Her hostess's were gnarled with arthritis, their skin wrinkled and their veins prominent as ropes. Her own, by contrast, were childish and unformed. Her fingernails, ordinarily bitten to the quick, had grown in during her long illness and were remarkably clean. She scarcely recognized them. Indeed, many things were strange, from the soft rose-coloured shawl around her thin shoulders to the long hair braided neatly down her neck. Maybe if she was this brand-new person she would be able to live in the present; maybe she could stop running away from the past. Besides, this woman had saved her life — did she not owe her the truth?

She took a deep breath, lay back down on the pillows, and began.

"My mother died of typhoid fever when I was four years old. She was ... not married. She was a simple housemaid, uneducated."

"But you loved her."

"Very much."

"And after she died?"

"My father brought me up because he thought it was his duty, not realizing how impossible it would be for his wife."

"Was your stepmother cruel to you?"

"She was always angry with me. She called me 'the bastard' or 'that ugly girl' and made it clear that I was not a real member of the family. But her oldest sons were kind; they let me sit in on their lessons. I loved my brother Daniel very much. He was my champion."

"Why didn't your father protect you?"

Esther couldn't resist the sympathy flooding into her from Madame Lévesque's hands. She found herself revealing things she had never told anyone else before.

"He was rarely home. Sometimes he returned late at night to find me sobbing about something vicious his wife had said to me. He always asked me to forgive her and to understand how hard things were for her. But even as a child I wondered why I was required to forgive her for things she did on purpose when she never forgave me for things that were not my fault."

"It is no wonder you ran away," Madame Lévesque said, gathering Esther into her arms as though to protect her from any future harm. "But things have changed, Esther. Here in Quebec you have people who care for you."

Esther shook her head and turned away, her shoulders shaking with the sudden onslaught of the grief she always tried to conceal. Madame Lévesque got up from the bed and returned with a dainty embroidered handkerchief. She waited quietly until the girl blew her nose and regained her composure before resuming.

"You know it's true, my dear. While you were sick, you had lots of visitors."

"I remember very little," Esther said, grateful for the change of subject.

"Madame Duplessis came often with that maid of hers, the one who squints."

"That was my friend Claire. And Marie-Thérèse, Monsieur Hocquart's housekeeper, came to see me too, didn't she?"

"She sat beside you for hours, praying for your recovery."

"There was also a man I didn't recognize. Quite handsome, with bright blue eyes."

"My youngest son, Joseph, visiting from Montreal. Perhaps you were less sick than we thought, if you were able to notice his good looks." Madame Lévesque smiled.

"Now you are embarrassing me."

"Well, you are at the age when you should be thinking about men."

"Please stop, Madame," Esther said. Her hostess was amused to see that she was blushing.

"Why? Are you really so different from other girls?"

"I suspect that there are others like me, who would rather have the wind in their sails than a baby in their belly."

"That may be," Madame Lévesque replied, laughing. "But few of them would have the courage to act on their desires."

"Why do girls always have to give up their dreams?" Esther asked, with a trace of her old spirit of defiance.

"Do you think that men can do whatever they want?"

"At least they are not prevented from doing things simply because they are men."

"There are other limitations people face, Esther."

"Such as poor health, or poverty?"

"Yes, or lack of education, or being the wrong race or religion. Like my darling husband."

"What do you mean?"

Madame Lévesque mumbled, almost too softly for Esther to hear, "It may be dangerous for all of us, but I thought you ought to know."

"Know what?"

"That you are not the only one who has needed to wear a disguise."

"I don't understand," said Esther, but even as the words left her mouth she realized that she did. The doctor's sadness and the cryptic comments he sometimes made began to make sense. The voice singing Sephardic ballads when she was sick had not been a feverish delusion as she'd assumed — it must have been him. He was the one who brought her here in the carriage. In her delirium she had failed to recognize the significance of that moment, which seemed so obvious to her now.

"But his name is Lévesque!"

"His grandfather's name was Cohen. It is a more or less literal translation."

Esther could not believe what she was hearing. "Are there any other Jews here?" she whispered.

"A few. But they live in hiding. I cannot tell the truth about Gabriel to anyone — not even my sisters or close friends like Madame Duplessis."

"Do your children know?"

"We waited until they were adults to tell them, worried they might otherwise endanger their father by some inadvertent comment."

"Would it not endanger them as well?" Esther asked, bewildered.

"I doubt it. My family, as you know, is quite prominent. We raised our children to be good Catholics and they are raising theirs the same way. I hope that by the time they are adults no one will care about their grandfather's religion."

Madame Lévesque smiled. "You know, Esther, I thought you would feel less solitary if I told you my secret. But now I realize that it was I who felt alone."

"Thank you for trusting me, Madame," Esther said, rising unsteadily from the bed to give her a fierce embrace. "I will never betray you."

"I know you won't, my dear. And besides," she laughed, "who would believe you?"

~

NOW THAT SHE WAS feeling better, Esther spent more and more time out of bed, taking her meals with the family and sitting outside in the sun to watch Madame Lévesque work. Her new hostess shared Madame Duplessis's passion for gardening and was still fit enough to indulge it, but having only a small plot, she cultivated flowers rather than fruits and vegetables. She was as tender with them as if they had been children, deadheading the spent roses and picking aphids off the new buds, clipping away extra branches and yellow or spotted leaves, working compost into the soil with a trowel. Although she was a wealthy woman with a houseful of servants, she insisted that gardening was not a chore but her greatest pleasure.

Madame Lévesque had reserved a special area for herbs, many of which were medicinal such as the lavender used upon Esther's infected wound. She had gained a reputation as a naturalist, following the work of the royal physician, Michel Sarrazin, in order to assist her husband's practice. She was very interested in aboriginal remedies and cultivated some of their ingredients as well: maidenhair fern to treat respiratory ailments, wintergreen for pains in the joints, purple coneflower for ague, bloodroot as an emetic, and ginseng as an all-purpose tonic. She also scraped spruce gum off trees to use as a salve for wounds and as a cure for diseases of the bladder. The advantage of local plants was that they were adapted to the climate, unlike European herbs; even rosemary, a perennial in France, rarely survived the challenge of a Canadian winter. She was forced to bring a small pot inside before the first frost and replant it in the spring with marjoram, basil, thyme, and dill seedlings. On the other hand, cultivating these tender herbs kept her garden alive indoors when the land was frozen. The foreign plants and the native ones balanced each other.

For Madame Lévesque, the most important principle in life was balance. She held that the balance in Quebec's four distinct seasons paralleled that of the body's four humours: winter was cold and wet like the phlegmatic humour; spring hot and wet like the sanguine; summer hot and dry like the choleric; autumn cold and dry like the melancholic. Esther, she was convinced, had been melancholic for years; coming to Canada in disguise had only made this worse, the suppression of her true character resulting in an excess of black bile. For this reason the septicaemia she had suffered at the hospital — far from being a punishment for her wickedness, as the nuns had insisted — had actually been purgative, cleaning the cold out of her body by means of a blazing fever the way one cleared virgin land by burning stumps. Now she was ready to start life anew.

"It's too bad you weren't here for the feast day of your namesake," Madame Lévesque remarked casually one day, as Esther followed her around carrying gardening tools and a basket.

"You celebrate Purim?" Esther replied, amazed. Though she had come to terms with the idea of the doctor being Jewish, there were few signs of observance in the family's daily life except for the way that he scraped the pork off his plate onto his wife's as soon as the servants left the room and stood silently praying, facing east, in the early morning. It was true that the family lit candles and drank wine on Shabbat, but since they did so nightly these practices did not stand out in any way. Anything else the doctor did he must have done alone and in secret.

"I don't myself, but Gabriel keeps the fast the day before — the better to get drunk during the festive meal."

Esther had to laugh at that. "Purim is my favourite holiday. Not because you are required to get drunk, though of course that part is fun, but because Esther has always been my inspiration."

"I thought so. In fact, I suspected you were Jewish as soon as I heard your name and learned that you had arrived here in disguise."

"Really? Then why did you send me to Madame Duplessis's house, where I had to pretend to pray to Jesus all the time?"

"I thought you two would be good for each other. She was lonely, and so were you." Madame Lésveque straightened up, groaning at the stabbing pain in her lower back. "Besides, one of the things I have learned from Gabriel is that God has many names; He does not mind which one you use in your prayers as long as your intentions are good. I myself would pray to any deity with the power to cure my arthritis."

"Poor Maman," said a man, coming into the garden with a travel-worn cloak and muddy boots.

"Joseph!" cried his mother, flinging her arms around his neck and kissing him. "When did you grow a beard?"

"It is the fashion in Montreal," he smiled. "But I will shave it off if it displeases you."

"No, don't; you look exactly like your father did at your age; even more handsome perhaps. But I am being rude. Do you remember Mademoiselle Brandeau, who was terribly ill the last time you visited us?"

"I am glad to see that you are recovered, Mademoiselle Brandeau," he said, bowing. "My parents were very concerned about you."

"Your parents saved my life, Monsieur," Esther replied, curtseying.

"Do not be so dramatic, Esther," Madame Lévesque said. "You are one of the family now."

And with one arm around the waist of her son and the other around Esther, Madame Lévesque led the two young people, laughing, into the house. She knew it was bad luck to wish too hard for things, but somehow she could not help feeling that things were unfolding as the universe intended.

THIRTEEN

"Uno año mas, un sehel mas."
(A year older, a year wiser.)

IT WAS A WARM August day. Even with all the windows open and the occasional breeze riffling the piles of paper on his desk, Hocquart found it necessary to strip to his shirt. Wet patches had spread under his armpits, beads of sweat rolled down his belly, and he had become uncomfortably aware that he stank. Another two hours of work, perhaps, and then he'd need a bath and change of clothes before dinner with Beauharnois.

He'd been putting off seeing the Governor General for weeks, knowing that their first topic of conversation was likely to be the fate of Esther Brandeau. His orders were clear: she must convert or be sent back to France immediately.

When the girl had still been mortally ill the subject had been moot, but now that she had recovered a decision had to be made. She could not stay at the Lévesques' house as though the question of her status had been resolved. He had probably been remiss in allowing Madame Lévesque to take her home in the first place, but the woman had insisted that if Esther stayed in the hospital she would die and Hocquart had never been able to refuse Madame Lévesque anything. She was a force of nature.

He glanced at the letter sitting on his desk, as yet unanswered. A letter he had received in June, on the first ship that arrived from France. Like everyone else, he had been waiting at the harbour that day with great anticipation. Some people were welcoming friends and relations; some receiving trade goods; ladies were looking forward to the latest fashions from Paris and gentlemen to new shipments of wine and brandy. The army awaited fresh recruits, tradesmen new apprentices. He himself was most anxious to receive not official correspondence but a large quantity of superior chocolate. The chocolate had indeed arrived, but so had this letter, confirming the information that Varin had received from his spies. Esther Brandeau was a Jew.

Ordres du Roy et Dépêches aux Colonies
21 April 1739

I do not know whether one can trust implicitly the declaration made by the so-called Esther Brandeau, who went out to Canada last year dressed as a boy on the vessel 'Saint Michel.'

However that may be, I have approved of your course in
placing her in the Hôpital Général at Quebec, and I shall be
very glad to hear of her conversion.

> — *From the Minister of the Marine to the Sieur*
> *Hocquart, Intendant of the Government of*
> *France in Quebec*

Damn. There must be some cologne around somewhere he could dab on; Marie-Thérèse would know where it was. He could not afford to smell bad in front of that peacock. And then it came throbbing back to him, like a toothache, that Marie-Thérèse had gone. It had taken him entirely by surprise when she had asked for his blessing. Who would have thought that such a homely woman, a woman thirty-six years of age, would receive an offer of marriage? Her new husband was respectable enough: a stout-hearted habitant, a widower with three daughters, farming a nice acreage on the Île d'Orléans. Apparently, they had struck up an acquaintance at the market while debating the merits of different kinds of cheese. Having grown up on a dairy farm, Marie-Thérèse was very knowledgeable about the subject. The farmer, who was a practical man, had discerned in her a hardworking woman who would make an excellent partner on his farm and mother to his children, and had proposed. If something so unlikely could happen to his housekeeper, Hocquart reflected wryly, perhaps there was still hope for him.

Marie-Thérèse had helped him find her replacement before she left, for he did not relish the prospect of interviewing a flock of clucking hens and then choosing the one he would have to look at and talk to for God only knows how long. Unfortunately, the best candidate for the job was a hatchet-faced widow named Madame Archambault. She did a good job of keeping the place in order — there was no more nonsense and waste from the other servants anymore — but in truth he wished for someone like Esther to keep him company: someone clever and entertaining who liked good food. But of course, Esther couldn't manage a household; the girl had no domestic skills at all.

At Marie-Thérèse's wedding, where he had been the guest of honour, she inquired politely how he was getting along. Having had more than his share of the potent local cider, he confessed his distaste for his new housekeeper. He wished she had found him someone who looked less like a hangman, someone more lively and interesting to be around. And, worst of all, no one in the kitchen could make a decent cup of chocolate anymore.

"Perhaps it is not too late to change that," Marie-Thérèse replied, looking fondly at her strapping new husband waltzing his youngest daughter around the room, the girl's dainty slippers perched on top of his big clumsy boots.

"What do you mean?" he asked.

"Monsieur Hocquart," she said hesitantly, recognizing the stiffening in his manner. "I could not help noticing how fond you were of Esther Brandeau. Well, she is all alone in the world and so are you. Maybe … maybe the two of you would be happier together?"

Fortunately for the Intendant, who was flushed with embarrassment and drink, the groom swung by with his giggling daughter and swept Marie-Thérèse away before he had to think of an answer. Almost immediately he called for his carriage and went home, grateful that no one else had overheard their conversation. But he found himself pondering what Marie-Thérèse had suggested.

Surely it was impossible?

He would first have to persuade Esther to convert to Catholicism, a task at which even the formidable Mother Claude had failed. On the other hand, he would be offering himself in return, which was a different kind of proposal than had ever been made to her before. She had nothing and no one; it was possible that marriage might appear a fair exchange, even if the husband were old and bald like him. They did have some things in common after all — they had the same taste in books and food. And similarity of taste was supposed to be a solid foundation for a domestic relationship.

Of course, there would be no way he could stay in Quebec if he wed Esther Brandeau; that much was obvious. Beauharnois would humiliate them both at every possible occasion and he would never be able to assert his authority among the man's followers. But why couldn't he start over with a new posting in some other corner of the Empire? With a wife such as her — young, charming, clever — he might actually rise further in the colonial administration. They would go somewhere less difficult to govern, somewhere warmer than New France: one of the prosperous sugar islands like Guadeloupe or Sainte Domingue perhaps. A place where she could recover her health swinging in a hammock all day, a place where they could eat exotic fruits, grow their own chocolate, bathe in a sparkling turquoise ocean. Esther had spoken often of how much she loved the ocean. Maybe he could tempt her with that prospect, if not with the prospect of having him as her husband.

He wandered over to a shelf and pulled down an atlas; thumbing through it he was gratified to see that the power of France spread across the globe. Not that he relished the thought of another long sea journey. But a thrill of excitement ran down his spine all the same. Reliable, dull Gilles Hocquart hadn't done anything unexpected in his whole life. He had simply laboured on diligently in the job his father had chosen for him, without asking himself whether he was happy, or lonely, or if, perhaps, he might have preferred a different way of life. Maybe he should have asked before, but at least he was asking now. And maybe it wasn't too late.

∼

"I AM SPEECHLESS," ESTHER said.

"Shall I take that as a good or a bad omen?" asked Hocquart.

The girl acknowledged his attempt at humour with a wry smile, then walked over to the window and stared off into the distance. Her movements were unexpectedly graceful and caught him off guard; somehow she seemed less encumbered by her clothes, more accustomed to walking in skirts, than he remembered. There was definitely something different about her. Her hair, of course, had grown much longer, and she now wore it combed over her high forehead and secured with a velvet ribbon, then tumbling down her back in long shiny waves. She had plucked and shaped her scraggly eyebrows, doubtless at the prompting of Madame Lévesque, who was nothing if not fashionable, and was wearing a pretty dress in a lilac colour that suited her complexion very well. In addition, she had gained weight since he had last seen her and looked less angular than before. All the ways Esther had changed made his proposal of marriage seem less absurd than he had feared it might, and gave him hope that she might be inclined to accept it.

The object of his silent scrutiny sighed, clasped her hands together as though to give herself strength, then finally responded, her back still to him, her gaze fixed on something outside.

"The last day I was living with Madame Duplessis, just before Monsieur Varin came to arrest me, I was telling her and my dear Madame Lévesque a tale of my adventures among the Tuareg, the blue men of the Sahara desert. I didn't get to finish it."

"What of it?" he said, bewildered by this apparent change of subject.

"Would you like to hear the rest of that story now? It is quite interesting." Finally she turned around to look at him. To his amazement, her eyes were full of tears.

"If it is that important to you, I will. You know how much I love your stories, Esther."

She turned away from him again, her gaze fixed once more on the window.

∼

IT TOOK ME A couple of months to recover my health and more to recover my spirits after the death of my guardian,

Monsieur Fourget, in the Sahara Desert. But my rescuers, a couple named Az'ar and Faghizza, tolerated my silent misery. Though from the outside they looked as different as chalk and cheese, he thin and solemn, she fat and merry, they were alike in their good hearts and in their profound generosity. They made no distinction between their own flesh and blood and me — whatever they had they shared: food, shelter, love. With them, I began to learn what it means to be truly human. And with them, I found a home.

Now, this home was in its own way a desert island, cut off from the rest of the world, with a peaceful rhythm and few occupants; a good place for me to recover my health. My hosts asked very little of me, but as I regained my strength I began to long for meaningful activity. It turned out that Faghizza was a revered healer among the villagers, so she offered to teach me her trade. This appealed greatly to me because my most fervent wish was to pay her and her husband back for their kindness. I began to learn the secret powers of the medicinal herbs she grew, how to lance infected wounds and bind broken bones, how to soothe the troubled minds and comfort the aching bodies of those who came to her for help. She said that I had good hands and a quick mind, and that I had been sent by God to be her helper and her adopted daughter.

One day a stranger, his blue eyes blazing from a sunburnt face, was carried into the village on a stretcher, delirious with snakebite. To my astonishment, the man spoke perfect French, even when he mumbled or shouted in his fits. Faghizza and I tended to his wound, which was severe, and it is no lie to say that we saved his life. When he recovered, we learned that he was a trader en route to the coast and that his name was Yousef — or at least, that was what he told us it was. This did not bother my hosts, accustomed as they were to people having but a single name, but it intrigued me, suggesting that he was travelling in disguise. I was so used to travelling in disguise myself that I felt an immediate affinity for the fellow. We were both strangers in a strange land, and he was full of entrancing tales of the places he had been and the wonders he had seen; I could listen to him for hours. My heart burned within my chest like that hot wind the Arabs call the *simoom*, until I finally recognized a passion I had never felt before.

~

"ENOUGH," HOCQUART INTERRUPTED ANGRILY. "You have made yourself quite clear. No *simoom* of love burns in your heart for me."

"But you are not in love with me either, Monsieur Hocquart," Esther protested.

"I thought that, with time, we could learn to love each other."

"We might learn to accept other. But you deserve better."

"I offer you marriage and you have the nerve to pretend that you are rejecting me for my own good?"

"Dear Monsieur Hocquart," she began. "It is precisely because you have always been so kind to me that I must reject your proposal."

"What do you mean?"

"You are a man with great responsibilities and therefore you need a wife who has been well brought up; someone who can run a household and knows how to behave in public. But I am not like that. I would bring you nothing but trouble."

There was a moment of silence while the Intendant absorbed her comments. It was hard for him to accept that the girl had responded to him as though they were equals rather than acknowledging his power over her. This behaviour, more than anything else that had happened during the year of Esther Brandeau's residence in Quebec, made him realize that religious conversion would not tame her fundamental independence; nothing would.

He sighed. "You realize that you have rejected your last chance to stay in New France."

"But I'm so happy living with Madame Lévesque," Esther said, panicking. "Please, Monsieur Hocquart, I beg of you. Don't send me away."

"Remaining here is no longer an option."

Hocquart walked over to the same window where Esther had been standing, trying to catch his breath. But the air outside was thick as soup and offered no relief for either his constricted lungs or his baffled mind. He was mortified to have made such an absurd proposal. How could he have been so reckless of his own reputation?

Nor did he relish the task ahead of him: arranging for Esther's passage home. The foolish girl was already sobbing as if her heart would break. He recognized belatedly that her facade of invulnerability was entirely that: a facade. Unable to bear her grief or his own humiliation a moment longer, he walked out the door without saying goodbye.

Although the thick stone walls of the Lévesque house kept

it relatively cool, outside the sun beat down, casting long noon-time shadows across the grass. A gaunt brown dog lay panting in the heat and a horse, his reins looped loosely around the fence, flicked his tail at a buzzing cloud of flies. It would be pleasant by the river, Hocquart supposed. Instead of trudging back to work he could go down there and watch the boats sailing back to France, or to the West Indies, or who knows where: more attractive places, places he would never go.

But after a few minutes of brisk walking, his pace slowed and his anger at being rejected began to cool. He realized, with some surprise, that he was more relieved than hurt. Perhaps he really was too old to change, after all.

～

27 September 1739, Quebec

Monsieur Pelissier, to whom I wrote about the adventures of the Jewish girl, Esther Brandeau, who arrived in this country last year disguised as a boy, has written me that she appears to be the bastard daughter of David Brandeau, a Jew of Bayonne, who told him that he has eight more children at home. She is so flighty that she has been unable to settle down, neither in the Hôpital Général nor in any of the other private homes in which I have placed her. The Warder of the prison finally took charge of her and keeps her there. She has not displayed consistently bad behaviour, although she is so capricious that she has been sometimes accommodating and other times resistant to the instructions which zealous ecclesiastics have tried to give her. I have no other option but to send her home. The Sieur Lafargue, captain of the ship Le Comte de Matignon de La Rochelle *has been charged with returning her to Monsieur Bellamy.*

— *From the Intendant Gilles Hocquart to the French Minister of the Marine.*

~

"OVER THERE," VARIN POINTED with grim satisfaction. "*Le Comte de Matignon de La Rochelle* is the ship that will take you back to Bayonne, where you belong."

Esther walked along beside him silently, her eyes downcast. They were accompanied by the two guards the King had ordered to watch over the girl on the voyage. Monsieur Hocquart did not think an armed escort was necessary but the last letter he received from His Majesty had insisted on it, assuring him that he would be recompensed for the expense. The girl was utterly passive, so there was nothing for the soldiers to do but carry her possessions: two bags of clothing and a few farewell gifts. Hocquart himself had given her a beautifully illustrated copy of *The Thousand and One Nights* and Madame Duplessis an edition of the letters of Marie de l'Incarnation. Madame Lévesque had given her a pair of candlesticks and several candles, that she might have light to read these books by. Marie-Thérèse, ever practical, had simply filled a handwoven Indian basket with food for the journey.

Naturally the Intendant was too busy to see her off, and the precise time of the girl's departure had been kept secret from the others so as to avoid unnecessary commotion. Varin was grateful for this; far too much attention had been paid to the sneaky little Jew already. He was relieved she wouldn't have the opportunity to make one last scene today.

She finally looked up to see where he was pointing. Her face became more animated. "A fine vessel indeed," she said. "Who is the captain?"

"The Sieur Lafargue."

"Is his name really Lafargue?"

"Yes."

Esther started to laugh, though her face was streaked with tears. She picked up her skirt in both hands and ran quickly up the gangplank, unaware, as usual, how much leg she revealed. The guards stumbled after her, burdened by her things. On the dock, a few men snickered and pointed, making rude comments; Varin told them to shut up and then called Esther's name, insisting that she come back.

"You are my prisoner!" he shouted, feeling foolish.

But the girl didn't glance back at him, or at the land that had been her home for the last year.

ACKNOWLEDGEMENTS

THE TALE-TELLER IS A fantasy improvised on a suggestive but poorly documented historical incident. Most of what we know about Esther Brandeau comes from the report filed by Jean-Victor Varin de La Marre, which follows in my translation. The original, as well as Intendant Gilles Hocquart's observations about the girl's year in Canada, are available in microfiche from the National Archives of Canada, series C11A–B, 71 and 72. Letters received in reply from France may be found in 68 and 71; excerpts from some of these are quoted in my novel as well.

In *The Tale-Teller*, the fact that Esther Brandeau was Jewish is revealed only in the spring of 1739, when communication with France resumed, rather than upon her arrival. I wasn't interested in writing a whole book of religious controversy. What intrigued me was Esther's character — what made her brave and foolhardy enough to run away and what made people in New France hold on to her until a direct order from the King forced them to send her home. That in reality she blurted out her true identity as soon as she was challenged influenced my interpretation of her as a fantastic storyteller rather than an intrepid adventurer. Someone so fearful of authority could never have passed as a boy for five long years, including a stint in jail.

Information about Varin, Hocquart, Governor General Beauharnois, and Mother Claude de la Croix comes from the *Dictionary of Canadian Biography.* The translations from the works of Marie de l'Incarnation are Joyce Marshall's from *Word from New France: The Selected Letters of Marie de l'Incarnation* (Toronto: Oxford University Press, 1967). The Wendat phrases spoken by Madame Duplessis are borrowed from the beautiful "Huron Carol" written by Saint Jean de Brébeuf. The story of the scholar who fell into the water has been freely adapted from that recounted in *Jewish Folktales,* as told by Pinhas Sadeh and translated from the Hebrew by Hillel Halkin (NY: Doubleday, 1989). And the Ladino proverbs known as "refranes" that introduce each chapter were found in *The Sephardic Tradition: Ladino and Spanish-Jewish Literature,* edited by Moshe Lazar and translated by David Herman (NY: W.W. Norton, 1972).

I am not alone in suspecting that there were some hidden Jews among Quebec's early settlers, as there were in all the other North and South American colonies. Rabbi Arthur A. Chiel, in an article for the Manitoba Historical Society published online at http://www.mhs.mb.ca/docs/transactions/3/jewishhistory. shtml, suggests that Marc Lescarbot, whose *Histoire de la Nouvelle-France* was published in 1609, was of Jewish descent, because Lescarbot demonstrated an unusual knowledge of Hebrew and attempted to prove that the First Nations were descendants of the ten lost tribes of Israel. More wide-ranging and scientific in its ambitions, the *anusim* project at http:// www.familytreedna.com/public/canadiananusim/default.aspx is currently seeking DNA proof that there were crypto-Jews among early immigrants. Corroboration may also be found in an interesting article by Jean-Marie Gélinas about his family's roots, posted online at http://www.gelinas.org. Both sources cite the registers of the "Saint-Office" (the French equivalent of the Inquisition) as evidence that the name "Lévesque" was considered Jewish at the time my story takes place.

Gélinas also provides commentary on, and links to, Pierre Lasry's 2001 novel about Esther Brandeau, *Une Juive en Nouvelle France,* published in English as *Esther: A Jewish Odyssey* in 2004. I deferred reading both Lasry's novel and *Esther,* by Sharon McKay, until after I completed my own book (having begun it before I was aware of Lasry's and before McKay's came out) and was relieved to discover that our interpretations of the girl's character were entirely different. For a fascinating exploration of the range of such interpretations throughout Canadian history, see Nathalie Ducharme, "Fortune critique d'Esther Brandeau, une aventurière en Nouvelle-France" (2004).

Joaquin's stories appeared in an earlier form in *The University of Windsor Review* 39.1 (2006) thanks to Marty

Gervais. For financial and moral support when it mattered, I am happy to acknowledge the Toronto Arts Council, the Ontario Arts Council, Cormorant Books, Dundurn Press, Black Moss Press, and Sumach Press. Martha Baillie, Rachel Klein, and Carolyn Smart were my first readers, and this book is much better for their advice. Helen Dunmore's encouragement has meant more than I can express. My agent, Alisha Sevigny of The Rights Factory, believed in Esther from the start, as did my amazing editor, Marc Côté, whose rigorous aesthetic pushed this story to be as good as I could make it, and whose own ancestors arrived in New France in 1637.

My biggest debt is to my husband Toan Klein and our children Jesse and Rachel, for filling my days with love and our trip to France with chocolate — the secret recipe for which was brought to the Pays Basques by Jews fleeing the Spanish Inquisition. These days, every town in the area has at least one *chocolatier* but few have any Jews. When Esther Brandeau lived in Bayonne, there were thirteen active synagogues. Now there are none.

There is, however, a synagogue in Quebec City.

REPORT FROM VARIN DE LA MARRE
TO THE AUTHORITIES IN FRANCE,
SEPTEMBER 15, 1738

Today, the fifteenth of September, one thousand seven hundred thirty-eight, Esther Brandeau, aged about twenty years, appeared before us, the Commissary of the Marine, charged with policing the maritime population of Quebec; the aforementioned girl embarked at La Rochelle disguised as a boy passenger under the name of Jacques Lafargue, on the ship Saint Michel *commanded by Le Sieur de Salaberry, and has declared herself to be Esther Brandeau, daughter of David Brandeau, a Jew by race, a merchant of St. Esprit in the diocese of Daxe, near Bayonne, and herself Jewish in religion. Five years ago her father and her mother sent her away from the said place on a Dutch boat captained by Geoffrey to send her to Amsterdam to her aunt and her brother, but the boat was lost on the sandbanks of Bayonne during the moon of April or May, one thousand seven hundred thirty-three. Luckily, she was brought to shore by one of the seamen, and she lodged with the widow Catherine Churriau who was living at Biarritz, then fifteen days later she left, dressed as a man, for Bordeaux where, in this capacity and under the name of Pierre Mausiette, she engaged on a ship commanded by Captain Barnard destined for Nantes; she returned on the same boat to Bordeaux where she re-embarked in the same disguise on a Spanish boat with Captain Antonio, sailing to Nantes; having arrived at Nantes, she deserted and went to Rennes, where she found employment as a boy with a tailor named Augustin; she stayed there for ten months, then from Rennes she went to Clisson where she entered the service of the Recollets as a domestic and errand boy, and she stayed three months at the convent, after which she left without warning to go to Saint Malo where she found sanctuary with a baker named Jeunesse living close to the Great Door, where she stayed five months offering certain services to the said Jeunesse, then she went to Vitré to investigate certain things. There, she found employment under the director of the Chapel, a captain of the Queen's Infantry, where she served for ten or eleven months as a lackey, then she left this place because her health did not permit her to continue serving the director of the Chapel who was always sick; the so-called Esther then returned near to Nantes, to a place named Noisel, where she was arrested for being a thief by the misfortune of being in the wrong place but she was let go after twenty-four hours because they saw that they had been mistaken. She then presented herself at La Rochelle, having taken the name of Jacques Lafargue she boarded as a passenger on the boat Saint*

Michel, at which point we asked the said Esther Brandeau to tell us the reason she disguised her sex this way for five years, to which she replied that, having been saved from shipwreck, she arrived in Bayonne and was taken to the house of Catherine Churriau as she told us before, and there she ate pork and other meats the use of which is forbidden among the Jews, and she decided therefore from this time on never to return to her father and mother but to partake of the same liberties as Christians. This and all the forgoing comprises the testimony of the so-called Esther Brandeau, witnessed by us at Quebec this day and compiled by the said Varin.